CALL

MR. FORTUNE

A SHORT STORY COLLECTION

H.C. BAILEY

Written by H.C. Bailey
1878 – 1961

First published in 1920
By Dutton

This edition published 2020
By Affordable Classics

CASE I:
THE ARCHDUKE'S TEA

MR REGINALD FORTUNE, M.A., M.B., B.CH. F.R.C.S., was having a lecture from his father.

"You only do just enough," Dr. Fortune complained. "Never brilliant. No zeal. Now, Reginald, it won't do. Just enough is always too little. Take my word for it. And do be attentive to the Archduke. God bless you!"

"Have a good time, sir," said Mr. Reginald Fortune, and watched his father settle down in the car (a long process) beside his mother and drive off. They were gone at last, which Reginald had begun to think impossible, and the opulent practice of Dr. Fortune lay for a month in the virgin hands of Reginald.

"Beautifully patient the mater is," Reginald communed with himself as he ate his third muffin. "Fretful game to spend your life waitin' for a man to get ready. Quaint old bird, the pater. Death-bed manner for a tummy-ache. Wonder the patients lap it up."

But old Dr. Fortune was good at diagnosis, and he had his reasons for saying that Reggie lacked zeal. At Oxford, at his hospital, Reggie did what was necessary to take respectable degrees, but no more than he could help. It was remarked by his dean that he did things too easily. He always had plenty of time, and spent it here, there, and everywhere, on musical comedy and prehistoric man, golf and the newer chemistry, bargees and psychical research. There was nothing which he knew profoundly, but hardly anything of which he did not know enough to find his way about in it. Nobody, except his mother, had ever liked him too much, for he was a self-sufficient creature, but everybody liked him enough; he got on comfortably with everybody from barmaids to dons.

He was of a round and cheerful countenance and a perpetual appetite. This gave him a solidity of aspect emphasized by his extreme neatness. Neither his hair nor anything else of his was ever ruffled. He was more at his ease with the world than a man has a right to be at thirty-five.

1

It is presumed that he had never wanted anything which he had not got. Old Dr. Fortune possessed a small fortune and a rich practice, and Reggie enjoyed the proceeds and proposed to inherit both. The practice lay in that pleasant outer suburb of London called Westhampton, a region of commons and a large park, sacred to the well-to-do, and still boasting one or two houses inhabited by what auctioneers call the nobility.

In Boldrewood, the best of these places, there lived at this moment in Reggie Fortune's existence the Archduke Maurice, the heir-apparent to the Emperor of Bohemia. You may remember that the Archduke came to live in England shortly after his marriage. It is, however, not true, as scandal reported, that his uncle the Emperor sent him into exile. There is reason to believe that the Archduchess, a woman equally vehement and beautiful, was not liked in several European courts. On her return from the honeymoon she made a booby trap for that drill sergeant of a king, Maximilian of Swabia, and for some weeks the Central Powers were threatening to mobilize. But she was a Serene Highness of the house of Erbach-Wittelsbach, which traces its descent to Odin, and had an independent realm of nearly two square miles, with parliament and army complete, and even the Emperor of Bohemia could not pretend that Maurice had married beneath him. History will affirm the simple truth that the Archduke and the Archduchess sought seclusion in England because they were bored to death by the Bohemian court, which was perpetually occupied in demonstrating that you can be very dull without being in the least respectable. The Archduke Maurice was a man of geniality and extraordinarily natural tastes. His garden—a long walk—a pint of beer in one of the old Westhampton inns made him a happy day. The Archduchess was not so simple, for she loved to drive her own car, a ferocious vehicle. But Archduchesses may not do that in Bohemia.

Reggie, having eaten all the muffins, lit his pipe and meditated on the cases left him by his father. Old Mrs. Smythe had her autumn influenza, and old Talbot Browne had his autumn gout, and the little Robinsons were putting in their whooping-cough. A kindly world! . . . He was dozing in the dark when the telephone bell rang.

Was that Dr. Fortune? Would he come to Boldrewood at once—at once? The Archduke had been knocked down by a motor-car and picked up unconscious.

"Poor old pater!" Reggie grinned, as he put his tools together. The pater would never forgive himself for being out of this. He loved a lord, did the pater, and since he had been called in to remove a fish bone from the archducal throat he could not keep the Archduke out of his conversation. The royal geniality of the Archduke, the royal disdain of the Archduchess—Dr. Fortune had been much gratified thereby, and Reggie was prepared to loathe their Royal Highnesses. Thank Heaven, the pater was safe on his holiday! If his head swelled so over an archducal fish bone, he would have burst over an archduke knocked down.

Reggie was practical, if without sympathy; he made haste in his neat way, and the sedate chauffeur of Dr. Fortune was horrified by instructions to let the car rip. The streets of Westhampton are not adapted to this. The district has tried hard to keep itself rural still, and its original narrow winding lanes remain ill-lighted and overhung by trees. Boldrewood stands high, and its grounds border upon Westhampton Heath, across which there is one lamp per furlong. Just as Reggie's car swung round to the heath it was stopped with a jerk.

"What's the trouble, Gorton?" Reggie said to the chauffeur.

Gorton was leaning sideways and peering into the gloom of the gutter. A gleam from the sidelight winked at a body which lay still. "Give me a turn," Gorton muttered. His face showed white. Reggie jumped out, but Gorton was quicker. "Lumme, it's the Archduke!" he said, and his voice went up high.

"Don't be futile, Gorton." Reggie bent over the body. "Get the lamps on him."

Gorton backed the car and the body came into the light. Its face was crushed. Gorton gasped and swallowed. "But it's not him neither," he muttered.

After a minute Reggie stood up. "He was a fine chap about an hour ago," he said gently.

"All over, sir?" Reggie nodded. "Some hog done him in?"

"As you say, Gorton. Running-down case. Big car. Took him in the back. Went over his head. But I don't see how he got into the gutter." He walked round the body, moved it a little, and picked up two matches— unusual matches in England—very thin vestas with dark blue heads. "Why did you think he was the Archduke, Gorton?"

3

"Such a big chap, sir. Not many his measure. And there's something about the make of the poor chap that's very like. But thank God's it's not the Archduke, anyway."

"Why?" said Reggie, who was without reverence for Archdukes. "Well, let's take him along."

They brought the dead man to the lodge at the main gates of Boldrewood, and there left him with a message to be telephoned to the police.

The hall at Boldrewood is in the Victorian baronial style, absurd but comfortable. Reggie was still blinking at the light when a woman ran at him. His first notion of the Archduchess Ianthe was vehemence. She came upon him, a great fur cloak falling away from her speed, panting, black eyes glowing, and then stopped short, and her pale face was distorted with passion. "Dr. Fortune! You are not Dr. Fortune!" she cried.

"Dr. Fortune, Junior, madame. My father is away, and I am in charge of his practice." She muttered something in a language he did not know, and looked as if she was going to kill him. His second notion of her was that she was wickedly beautiful. A Greek perfection in the pale face, but, Lord, what a temper! The daintiest grace of body, but it moved and quivered like a whip lash.

"My dear Ianthe!" A man came smiling from behind the screen by the fire. He was tall and slight and dandyish: a lot of colour in his clothes, an odd absence of colour in him. A bright blue tie with an emerald in it, a bright blue handkerchief hanging half out of the pocket of the silver-grey coat. But his face had a waxy pallor, his hair, his moustache, and little pointed beard were so fair that they looked like patches of paint on a mask. "We are much obliged by Dr. Fortune's coming so quickly."

The Archduchess whirled round. "He is too young," she said in German. "Look at him. He is a boy."

"I beg your pardon, madame," said Reggie in the same language. "May I see the patient?"

The man laughed. "I am sure we have every confidence in your skill, Dr. Fortune." All the laughter was smoothed out of his face. "And your discretion," he said in a lower voice. "I am the Archduke Leopold. You may be frank with me. And rely upon my help."

Reggie bowed. "How did the accident happen, sir?"

4

The Archduke turned to his sister-in-law. "You know that I do not know," she cried. "I was out in the car."

"As my sister says, Dr. Fortune, she was out in the car." The Archduke paused. "She drives herself. It is with her a little passion. My brother was out walking alone."

"Those long walks! How I hate them!" the Archduchess broke out.

"Again, it is with him a little passion. Well, he did not come back. I grew anxious. I am staying here, you understand. My sister was late too. I sent out servants. My brother was found lying in the road not far from the gate of the lodge. He remains unconscious. I fear – –" He spread out his hands.

"You – you always fear!" the Archduchess cried. They exchanged glances like blows.

"May I go up, madame?" Reggie said solemnly. She whirled round and rushed away.

"The Archduchess is much agitated," said the Archduke.

"It is most natural," Reggie murmured.

"Most natural. Pray follow me, Dr. Fortune. I will take you to my brother."

The Archduke Maurice lay in a room of austere simplicity. A writing-table, a tiny dressing-table, three chairs, and a narrow iron bed were all its furniture. Only three small rugs lay on the floor. At the head of the bed a man stood watching. The Archduchess was on her knees, her face pressed to her husband's body, and she sobbed violently.

The Archduke Leopold looked at Reggie, made a gesture towards her, and said, "My dear Ianthe!"

She looked up flushed and tear stained.

"I beg your pardon, madame. This is dangerous to the patient," Reggie said.

She gave a stifled cry and rushed out of the room.

The Archduke Leopold seemed to intend to stay, but in a moment the voice of the Archduchess was heard calling for him. "Better go to her, sir. Keep her out of here," Reggie said, and turned to his patient. It was obvious that the Archduke did not relish so brusque an order. But the passionate voice was not to be denied.

5

The man by the bed and Reggie took each other's measure. "English?" said Reggie.

"Yes, sir. Holt, I am. The Archduke's valet."

"You undressed him?"

"Yes, sir. Was that wrong?"

"Depends how you did it." Reggie began his examination. The Archduke Maurice was a big man. That is a habit in his family. He had their fairness, but even in coma his cheeks showed more colour than his brother Leopold's, and his yellow hair and beard had a reddish glow. A bold, honest face with plenty of brow. Reggie went over his body with an anatomical enthusiasm for so splendid a specimen.

"Get me some warm water, will you?" Holt went out of the room. Reggie bent over the broad chest. From it, from just above the heart, he drew out a thin sliver of steel. He made a face at it and put it away. Holt came back, and there was sponging and bandaging.

"You washed him before, I see. Anyone else touched him but you?"

"Only carrying him, sir. I've been with him the whole time. I found him."

"Oh. Lying on his face, I suppose?"

"No, sir. On his back. Just like he is now."

"Oh. Notice anything?"

"No, sir, I wish I had. I'd like to have the handling of the bounder that did it."

"Well, well, we mustn't get excited. Preserve absolute calm, Holt. He's well liked, is he?"

"Why, sir, we'd do anything for him. He — oh, he's a gentleman."

"Quite so. You mustn't leave him a moment. No one — see, no one — is to come into the room. I'll be back soon."

"Very good, sir. Beg pardon, sir." The good Holt flushed. "What's the verdict?"

"It's not all over yet!" Reggie went downstairs.

And it appeared to him that he interrupted the Archduke and the Archduchess in a quarrel. But the Archduke was very pleased to see him, effusive in offering a chair, and so forth. Reggie was not gratified. "I must have nurses, sir," he announced. "I should like another opinion."

"You see!" the Archduchess cried. "It is as I told you. This boy!"

6

"The Archduchess is naturally anxious," the Archduke apologized. "By all means nurses. But another opinion—you must have confidence in yourself, my good friend."

"I have. But I want Sir Lawson Hunter to see the case."

The Archduke shrugged. "It is serious then, Dr. Fortune? We do not wish a great noise. Is it not so, Ianthe?"

"I would give my soul to be quiet," she cried.

"Quite," said Reggie.

"Very well. Discretion, then, you understand, my good friend."

"I'll telephone to Sir Lawson at once."

"Indeed? It is serious, then?"

"It's a bad concussion." Reggie bowed and made for the door.

"You—Dr. Fortune——" the Archduchess cried. "Will he—what will happen?"

"There's no reason we shouldn't hope, madame," Reggie said, and paused a moment watching them. Emotion plays queer tricks with faces. They were both in the grip of emotions.

Sir Lawson Hunter is rather fat and his legs are rather short. His complexion is greyish and his eyes look boiled. People call him dyspeptic, though his capacious stomach has never known an ache: or imagine that he drinks, though alcohol and physicians are his chief abominations. His European reputation as a surgeon has been won by knowing his own mind.

Reggie met him at the door and took him upstairs before that puzzling pair, the Archduke and the Archduchess, had a sight of him. "Glad you could come, sir. It's an odd case."

"Every case is odd," said Sir Lawson Hunter.

"He was knocked down by a car. The—"

"If he was, I can find it out for myself. Damme, Fortune, don't bias me. Most unprofessional. That's the worst of general practice. You fellows must always be saying something."

Reggie held his peace. He knew Sir Lawson's little ways, having been his house surgeon. The faithful Holt was turned out of the room. Sir Lawson Hunter went over the senseless body with his usual speed and washed his hands.

"Splendid animal," he remarked. "They run to that, these Pragas. I remember his uncle's abdominal muscles. Heroic. Well. He was walking. A big car driven fast hit him from behind on the right side, fractured two ribs, and knocked him down. Impact of his head on the road has caused a serious concussion. That car should have stopped."

Reggie smiled. "Oh, one of the odd things is that it didn't."

"There's a damned lot of road hogs about, my boy." said Sir Lawson heartily. He was himself fond of high speed. "Well. They sent out, I suppose. Found him lying on his face unconscious."

"No, sir."

"What?" Sir Lawson jumped.

"He was lying on his back."

"Oh, that's absurd."

"Yes, sir. But I've seen his valet who found him."

"These fellows have no observation," Sir Lawson grunted, but there was some animation in his boiled eye. "Damme, Fortune, he ought to have been on his face."

"Yes, sir."

"Miracles don't happen."

"No, sir."

"Now these abrasions on the legs. As if the car had been driven at him again while he lay. A queer thing. Or have there been two cars at him?"

"And there is this too, sir." Reggie held out the sliver of steel.

"I saw the puncture. I was coming to that. Humph! Whoever put this in meant business."

"And didn't know his job. It slipped along the bone and missed everything."

Sir Lawson turned the thing over. "A woman's hatpin. About half a woman's hatpin."

"Fresh fracture. Broke as it was pushed in."

"They're a wild lot," said Sir Lawson, and smiled. "You have no nerves, Fortune?"

"I believe not, sir."

"This ought to be the making of you. You want shaking up. You must stay in the house. By the way, who's in the house?"

"The Archduchess, of course ‒ ‒"

8

"Ianthe. Yes. Aunt's in a mad-house. Ianthe. Yes. Crazy on motoring. Drives her own car. And have you see Ianthe — since?" Sir Lawson nodded at the body on the bed.

"She is very excited."

"Is she really?" Sir Lawson laughed. "Is she, though? How surprising!"

"She is surprising, sir."

"What? What? Be careful, my boy. Handsome creature, isn't she?"

"Yes, sir." Reggie declined to be amused. "The Archduke Leopold is staying with them."

"Leopold. He's the dandy entomologist. He's tame enough. Well, he's the head of the house after this fellow. Better tell him." He blinked at Reggie. "You have nurses you can trust? Well, we'll stay in the room till one comes, my boy. Our friend of the hatpin won't miss a chance. These Royal families they're a criss-cross of criminal tendencies. Hohenzollerns, Hapsburgs, Pragas, Wittelsbachs — look at the heredity."

"There was another running-down case here tonight. The man was killed — fractured skull. He was left on the road too. And another queer thing — he was much the same build as the Archduke Maurice."

"Good Gad!" Sir Lawson was startled out of his omniscient manner, an event unknown in Reggie's experience. "There's something devilish in it, Fortune. One murder — the wrong man dead — and then try again at once the same way. Imagine the creature looking at that poor dead wretch and jumping on the car again to drive it on at the other man. Diabolical! Diabolical!"

"I don't think I have much imagination, sir," said Reggie, who was not impressed by ineffective emotion.

There was a gentle tap at the door, a nurse came and was given her instructions, and the two men went down to the Archduke Leopold.

He had changed his clothes. He was now in a claret-coloured velvet which did violence to his complexion and his pale beard. He sat in the smoking-room with a book on the entomology of Java and a glass of eau sucrée. He smiled at them and waved them to chairs.

"I have to tell you, sir, that your brother lies in grave danger," said Sir Lawson.

Reggie looked at him sideways.

"Ah, the concussion! It is serious, then? I am deeply distressed."

"The concussion is most serious. There's another matter. In your brother's chest above the heart, at which it must have been aimed, we have found—this."

"Mon Dieu! It is a hatpin—a woman's hatpin. But it is incredible! It is murder."

"Attempted murder."

"But what do you suggest, sir? Do you accuse someone?"

"Not my function. That pin was driven at your brother's heart by someone. Can you tell me anymore, sir?"

The Archduke buried his face in his hands. "I will not believe it," he muttered—"I will not believe it." After a little he controlled himself. "Gentlemen, you have a right to my confidence. I will tell you everything. I trust you to do all that is possible for my poor brother and for the honour of our family, which to him, as to me, is dearer than life. You know that he is the heir to the throne of Bohemia. My uncle, the Emperor, has long been vexed with his living in England. I came here to persuade my brother to go back to his country. My poor brother had made his home here at the wish of the Archduchess, who dislikes the duties of royalty. He was passionately, madly, in love with her. But, alas! In these love marriages there is often difficulty. They were not of the same mind upon many things, and the Archduchess is of a vehement temper. I fear—but you will forgive me if I say no more. I take one small thing. My brother loved to go walking. The Archduchess is passionately fond of her motor-car, drives it herself, and loves wild speed. My brother detested motor-cars. I fear that my coming gave them cause for fresh quarrels. My brother was ready to go back to Bohemia. The Archduchess was violently opposed to it. I confess to you, gentlemen, I have feared some scandal, some madness. I thought she would leave him. But this—it is appalling."

"The Archduchess was out in her motor-car tonight?" Sir Lawson said.

"Yes. Yes. It is true. But this—must we think it?"

"We have to think of nothing but our duty to our patient," said Sir Lawson.

The Archduke grasped his hand. "You are right. I thank you. I shall not forget your fidelity."

The Archduchess whirled into the room. She, as Reggie remarked, had not cared to change her clothes. She had not even touched her hair, which was escaping in a wild disorder from under her hat. "They will not let me see him," she cried. "Leopold — —"

"It is by my instructions, madame," Sir Lawson said. "I am responsible for the Archduke's safety."

She bit her lip. "Is he so hurt?" she said unsteadily.

"He lies in very grave danger, madame. I permit no one in his room."

She stared at him, her throat quivering, her great eyes bold and bright. Then with a little shrug she turned away and, plucking at the gold things which jingled from her waist, took out a cigarette and lit it. Reggie saw one of those foreign matches with the violet heads.

Sir Lawson made his bow, and Reggie went with him to his car. "Why did you tell them that the Archduke was in grave danger?" he said.

"He'll be safer if they believe he is going to die," said Sir Lawson.

"Oh, do you think so?" said Reggie, as the car shot away.

Then he made an excellent supper and slept sound.

He found his patient peaceful in the morning. No sign of consciousness yet, but more colour in the cheeks, a deeper breathing and a stronger pulse, more warmth. "The Archduchess has come twice in the night to ask about him, doctor," the nurse said. "I told her he was no better."

"Did she make a noise?" Reggie frowned.

"No, she was very good."

Reggie went out to take the air, and the air is not bad on the Westhampton heights. He made a good pace under the great beeches of Boldrewood, and came out on the open road across the heath. Just there he had found the dead man. A dull red stain could still be seen. It was farther on that the Archduke was struck. Just beyond the turn to Brendon. He found the place. There was a loosening of the road, as if a heavy car had been brought up sharply or made a violent swerve. He walked to and fro scanning the ground. Another of those foreign matches.

He was just picking it up when a motor-car stopped a few yards away. Two men jumped out and came towards him. One was middle aged and singularly without distinction. The other had a youthful and very jaunty air, and it was only when he came near that Reggie saw the fellow was old enough to be his father. An actor's face, with that look of calculated expression, and an actor's way of dressing, a trifle too emphatic. His present part was the gay young fellow.

11

"Dr. Fortune, I think?" He smiled all over his face.

"I am Dr. Fortune."

"Reconstructing the crime, eh? Oh, you needn't be discreet. I'm Lomas—Stanley Lomas—Criminal Investigation Department, don't you know? Sir Lawson Hunter came round to me last night. Patient's doing well, I see. That's providential. Just a moment—just a moment." He skipped away from Reggie to his companion, and they went over the ground. But Reggie thought them very superficial. Lomas skipped back again. "He didn't bleed, then. The other man did, though—the man you found."

"In the middle of the road. And I found him dead in the gutter."

"It's quaint what the criminal don't think of. I'm surprised every time. Did you find anything here?"

Reggie held out his match. "There were two more like that by the other man."

Lomas turned it over. "Belgian make. You buy them all over the Continent, don't you know."

"The Archduchess carries them."

"Now, that's very interesting. If you don't mind I'll walk up to the house with you." Upon the way he praised the beauties of nature and the quality of the morning air.

As they came to the door of Boldrewood a big car passed them with the Archduchess driving alone. Lomas put up his eyeglass. "She's not overcome with grief, what?"

"Not quite."

"Might be bravado, don't you know."

"I don't know."

"It takes some of them that way," Lomas said pensively. He turned on the steps of the house and looked after the car as it wound in and out among the beeches. "Striking woman. Yes. I'll come up to your room, if you don't mind."

"I thought you wanted to say something," Reggie said.

Lomas did not answer till they were upstairs. "Well, no. Not to say anything," he resumed, and lit a cigarette. "I want another opinion, as you fellows say. Sir Lawson Hunter has made up his mind."

"Oh, he always does that."

12

Lomas lifted an eyebrow. "Well, look at it. Somebody in a car laid for our Archduke. The other poor devil was cut down by mistake. And the somebody had nerve enough to go on. That's striking. The Archduchess comes of pretty wild stock. In love or out of love she wouldn't stick at a trifle. You find her matches by each body. You find a hatpin in the Archduke. That's a blunder, what? Yes, but it's a woman's blunder. She finds he isn't quite dead after all her trouble, she is desperate, and — *voilà*." He made a gesture of stabbing.

"So you've made up your mind too, Mr. Lomas?"

Lomas blew smoke rings. "I'm wasting your time, doctor. I want to know — has it occurred to you — the Archduchess and the Archduke Leopold — working it together? If she's fallen in love with Leopold. That straightens it out, don't you know."

"Guess again," Reggie said.

Lomas lit another cigarette. "Well, that's what I want to know. You saw them together just after the crime." He lifted an eyebrow.

"Nothing doing," said Reggie.

"I'm afraid so. I'm afraid so. It's a disturbing case, doctor. Nothing doing, as you say. If I had all the evidence in my hands, I expect there's no one I could touch. You can't indict royalty. The Archduke's smash — well, let's say it's all in the family. But this poor devil they killed! Who's to pay for him? These royal dagoes come over and run amuck on an English road, and I can't touch them. Disheartening, what? That's the trouble, doctor."

Reggie nodded and, as his breakfast made its appearance, Lomas rose to go. He would not have even coffee. "Better get busy, don't you know. We must see if we can put the fear of God into them. If they'll go scurrying back to Bohemia it's the best way out." He skipped off, his jauntiness put on again like a coat.

Reggie was standing at the window with his after-breakfast pipe when the Archduchess brought her car back. She was very pale in spite of the morning air, and her face had grown haggard. "Something'll snap," Reggie was saying to himself, when a voice behind him said aloud, "Nice car, sir." He jumped round and saw standing at his elbow the insignificant little companion of Mr. Lomas. "After all, there's nothing like an English car," said the little man.

"Oh. You've noticed that?" Reggie said. "You do notice something, then?"

"Of course we aren't gifted, sir. But we're professional. Something in that, don't you think? Yes, sir, as you say: we have noticed something. It was a foreign car, and foreign tyres did the trick last night. And the Archduchess drives English. And yet—did you know we had the other half of the hatpin? I picked it up last night." He held out a scrap of steel with a big head of wrought silver. "German work, they tell me."

"Viennese," Reggie said.

"You know everything, sir. Such a convenience. But Vienna being quite near Bohemia, as I've heard—looks awkward, don't it?"

"Is that what you came to say?"

"Not wholly, sir. No. I am Superintendent Bell. Mr. Lomas sent me to you. He considered you might find it convenient to have someone in the house who could keep an eye open."

"Very kind of Mr. Lomas."

There was a tap at the door. The Archduke Leopold's valet appeared. The Archduke Leopold was much surprised that Dr. Fortune had not brought him news of the patient. The Archduke Leopold desired that Dr. Fortune would come to him immediately.

"Really?" Reggie said. "Dr. Fortune's compliments to the Archduke, and he is much occupied. He can give the Archduke a few moments."

The valet, having the appearance of a man who has never been so surprised in his life, retired.

"It's a gift," Superintendent Bell murmured. "It's a gift, you know. I never could handle the nobs."

Reggie began to get together some odds and ends: a bottle full of tiny white tablets, a graduated glass, a jug of water, a hypodermic syringe. "You'd better clear out, you know," he said to Superintendent Bell.

"Will he come?"

"He'll come all right," Reggie said, and took off his coat. When he turned, Superintendent Bell had vanished.

"Just setting the stage, sir?" said a voice from behind the curtain.

"Confound your impertinence," Reggie growled. "Here — —"

But the Archduke came in. He was now a decoration in a russet brown. "You are very mysterious, Dr. Fortune," he complained. "I expect more frankness, sir."

"My patient is my first consideration, sir."

"I desire that you will consider my anxieties. Well, sir, how is my brother?"

"You may give yourself every hope of his recovery, sir."

The Archduke looked round for a chair and was some time in finding one. "This is very good news," he said slowly, and slowly smiled. "*Mon Dieu*, doctor, it seems too good to be true! Last night you told me to fear the worst."

"Last night—was last night, sir," Reggie said. "This morning we begin to see our way. All the symptoms are good. I believe that in a few hours the patient will be able to speak."

"To speak? But the concussion? It was so dangerous. But this is bewildering, doctor."

"Most fortunate, sir. You might talk of the hand of Providence. Well, we shall see what we shall see. He may be able to tell you something of how it all happened. You'll pardon me, I'm anxious to prepare the injection." He dropped a tablet in the glass and poured in water. "Fact is, this ought to make all the difference. Wonderful things drugs, sir. A taste of strychnine—one of these little fellows—and a man has another try at living. Two or three of 'em—just specks, aren't they?—sudden death. Excuse me a moment. I must take a look at the patient."

He was gone some time.

When he came back the Archduke was still there. "All goes well, doctor?"

"I begin to think so."

"I must not delay you. My dear doctor! If only your hopes are realized. What happiness!" He slid out of the room.

Reggie went to the table and picked up the glass of strychnine solution. From behind the curtain Superintendent Bell rushed out and caught his arm. "Don't use it, sir," he said hoarsely. Superintendent Bell was flushed.

"Don't be an ass," said Reggie. He put the glass down, took up the bottle of tablets, turned them out on a sheet of paper, and began to count them.

"Good Lord!" said Superintendent Bell. "You laid for him, did you? What a plant!"

"You know, you're an impertinence," Reggie said, and went on counting.

"I'll get on to Mr. Lomas, sir," said the Superintendent humbly.

"Don't you telephone or I'll scrag you."

"Telephone? Not me. I say, sir, you're some doctor." He fled.

Reggie finished his counting and whistled. "He did himself proud," said he. "The blighter!" He shot the tablets back into their bottle, found another bottle and poured into it the solution, and locked both away. "Number one," he said, with satisfaction. "Now for number two." He went off to his patient and spent a placid half-hour chatting with the day nurse on dancing in musical comedy. But it was hardly half an hour before the Archduchess tapped at the door.

Reggie opened it. "This way, if you please, madame." He led the way to his room. "I have something to say." She stood before him, fierce, defiant, and utterly wretched. "I can promise you that the Archduke will recover consciousness."

She caught at her breast. "He—he will live?" It was the most piteous cry he had ever heard.

"He will live, madame!"

She trembled, swayed, and fell. Reggie grasped at her, took her in his arms, and put her in a chair and waited frowning. . . . She panted a little and began to smile. Then faintly, softly, "No, no. No more now. Ah, dearest." It was in her own language. She opened heavy eyes. "What is it?"

"The Archduke has spoken, madame. He said—your name."

Then she began to cry and, holding out both hands to Reggie, "Let me go to him—please—please."

"Not now. Not yet. He must have no emotions. You will go to your room and sleep."

"You—you are a boy." She laughed through her tears, and thrust her hands into Reggie's.

"I beg your pardon, madame," Reggie said stiffly. The creature was absurdly adorable.

16

"You? Oh—Englishman." It was made plain to him that he was expected to kiss her hand. He did it like an Englishman. Then the other was put to his lips.

He cleared his embarrassed throat. "I must insist, madame, you will say nothing of this to anyone. It's necessary the household should suppose the Archduke still in danger."

"Why?" A spasm crossed her face. "You are afraid of Leopold!"

"And you, madame?" Reggie said.

"Afraid? No, but" —she shuddered —"but he is not a man."

"Have no anxieties, madame. I have none," Reggie said, and opened the door. Then, "She's a bit of a dear," he said to himself, and rang for his lunch.

Four times that afternoon the Archduke Leopold sent to ask for news of his brother, and each time Reggie answered that the patient was much the same. "Leopold will be doin' some thinking," Reggie chuckled. "Happy days for Leopold."

Towards tea-time the Hon. Stanley Lomas arrived jauntier than ever.

"Well, doctor, been enjoying yourself, what?" He shook hands heartily. "Best congratulations and all that. Sound scheme. Ve —ry sound scheme. Well, I expect you'll be glad to be rid of Leopold, what? I conceive I can put the fear of God into him now. Free hand, don't you know. Let's take him on."

It was announced to the Archduke Leopold that the Hon. Stanley Lomas of the Criminal Investigation Department desired to confer with him. The Archduke, who was drinking tea, was pleased to receive Mr. Lomas. He also received Reggie. "Dr. Fortune? You have something to tell me?"

"There is no change, sir."

"No change yet! And you gave me such hopes this morning. These are anxious hours, Mr. Lomas."

"I can imagine it, sir. But I hope to relieve some of your anxieties. I believe we shall discover who was responsible for last night's outrage."

"So! And so soon! But you are wonderful, you English police. You will sit down, Mr. Lomas." He looked at Reggie, whose lingering naturally surprised him. "Is there anything more, Dr. Fortune?"

"Dr. Fortune is part of my evidence, sir," said Lomas.

"Is it possible? But you interest me — you interest me exceedingly. Permit me one moment." He slid out of the room.

Lomas turned in his chair and lifted an eyebrow at Reggie, who was settling his tie before an old Italian mirror. "Probably gone to change his clothes," Reggie said. "He's only worn one suit to-day."

A footman brought in more tea-things, and a moment after the Archduke came back.

"I am all impatience, Mr. Lomas. But pray take a more comfortable chair. Dr. Fortune — I recommend the chair by the screen. Let me give you some tea." He was all smiles.

"Have you made arrangements to leave England, sir?" Lomas said sharply.

"Mr. Lomas!"

"You have time to catch the mail to-night."

"I hope that I do not understand you, sir. You appear insolent."

"Oh, sir, there will be no delicacy in handling the affair. You went to Dr. Fortune's room this morning." The Archduke gave a glance at Reggie, who sat intent on stirring his tea. "He was preparing an injection of strychnine for his patient."

"Hallo, what's that?" Reggie cried, and nodded at the window. "Oh, I suppose it's the car, Lomas. Your fellows will have found her and brought her round."

"The car, sir?" the Archduke said, and Lomas put up his eyeglass.

"The car that did the deed."

The Archduke slid across to the window. Lomas, too, stood up and looked out. They turned and stared at Reggie, who was sipping his tea. Lomas frowned. "There's nothing there, Fortune."

The Archduke smiled. "Dr. Fortune has hallucinations," and he pulled out his handkerchief and dabbed his face, sat down, and drank his tea in gulps.

"We'll keep to the point, if you please." Lomas was annoyed. "Dr. Fortune told you that two of his strychnine tablets would kill a man. He went out of the room. While he was gone you dropped half a dozen tablets into the injection prepared for your brother. I have to demand, sir, that you leave England by the next boat."

The Archduke burst out laughing. "The good Dr. Fortune! As you have seen, he has hallucinations. He hears what is not, dreams what never was. But if I were a policeman, Mr. Lomas, I should not make Dr. Fortune a witness. You become ridiculous."

"He is not the only witness, sir. One of my men was behind the curtain."

The Archduke poured himself out another cup of tea. "May I give you some more, Dr. Fortune? No? I fear you are malicious, my friend." He laughed a little. "And you, sir. We sometimes find a policeman corrupt in our country. We do not permit him to trouble us."

"You brought a German car into England, sir," Lomas said. "Where is that car?"

"Your spies do not seem very good, Mr. Lomas. Come, sir, enough of this. I— —" The Archduke started from his seat with a cry. His body was bent in a bow. A horrible grin distorted his face. He fell down and was convulsed. . . . He gasped; his pale cheeks became of a dusky blue. He writhed and lay still. . . .

"So that's that," Reggie said. "I wondered what he wanted with half a dozen."

"What is it?" Lomas muttered.

"Oh, strychnine poisoning. He's swallowed a grain or so."

"My God! Can you do anything?"

Reggie shrugged. "He's as dead as the table." . . .

After a while, "Well! It's a way out," Lomas said. "But I can't understand the fellow."

"Oh, I don't understand it all," Reggie admitted. "He was out to kill his brother. That meant being Emperor. But why kill him now more than before? And the Archduchess. She is straight enough, I know. But just how she was to this fellow I don't see."

"There's not much in that," Lomas said. "Maurice couldn't stand the Court, and it was common talk he meant to resign the succession. While he was quiet over here in England Leopold felt safe. But lately they tell me Maurice has been making up his mind to go back. Duty to his country, don't you know? The Archduchess was strong against it. She hates all the business of royalty. But Maurice is a resolute sort of fellow even with a woman. Leopold came over to see what he could do. I suppose he set the

Archduchess on to make Maurice give up the idea and stay quiet. They worked together—or that's the notion at the Bohemian Embassy. She's a gipsy, what, but she's straight. She is not in this. It wasn't her car. Well, when Leopold found there was nothing doing he set about the murder. He was a bad egg, don't you know? There was a woman in Rome—they kicked him out there. But it was a sound scheme. He had it all straight—except the wrong tyres on his car. Good touch, the hatpin. Seemed like a woman in a rage. He knew a lot about women—one kind of woman."

There was a tap at the door. The two walked forward.

"Sir Lawson Hunter, sir." The footman tried in vain to see the Archduke.

"Yes, bring him up," Reggie said.

Sir Lawson bustled in. "New case for you, sir." The two men moved apart and Sir Lawson saw the body.

"Poisoned himself. Taken strychnine," Lomas said.

"Oh, don't bias him," said Reggie. "He doesn't like that."

"Good Gad!" Sir Lawson's eyes bulged.

"Yes, that beats me, Fortune." Lomas waved his hand at the body. "I would have sworn he hadn't the pluck."

"Oh, he hadn't. He meant it for me. I changed the cups."

"You— —" Lomas stared at him. "That was when you heard the car!"

"That was why I heard the car."

"And you let him take the dose!"

"Yes. Seemed fair. You see, I picked up that poor fellow he smashed last night."

"Good Gad!" said Sir Lawson.

The footman was again at the door. Dr. Fortune was wanted at the telephone. "There's one here, isn't there? Put me through." The footman, hardly able to speak at the sight of the dead Archduke, retired gulping.

The bell rang. Reggie took up the receiver. "Yes. Yes. At once," and he put it down. "I must be going. Serious case. Mrs. Jones's little girl may have German measles."

CASE II:
THE SLEEPING COMPANION

BIRDIE screamed like a sea-gull and leapt on to the stage. The audience rumbled the usual applause, and Dr. Reginald Fortune put up his opera-glasses. He considered himself a connoisseur in the art of music halls, and Birdie Bolton was unique and bizarre. She was no longer young, and had never been pretty. A helmet of black hair, a gaunt face which never smiled, a body as lean as a boy's, which sometimes slouched and sometimes jerked — such were her charms. She wore nothing much above the waist but diamonds, and below it barbaric flounces in a maze of colour. She began to sing in a voice wildly unfit for the strange creature she looked — a small, sweet voice — and what she sang was a simple ditty about her true love forsaking her. And then she went mad. There was a shrieking chorus — can you imagine a steam whistle playing rag-time? — and a dance of weird, wild vehemence. The lean body was contorted a dozen ways at once, the long white arms whirled and stabbed. She seemed to be a dozen women fighting, and each of them a prodigy of force. It was not a pretty dance, but it had meaning.

Birdie sank down panting on her crazy rainbow flounces and nodded at the audience which thundered at her.

Dr. Reginald Fortune shut up his opera-glasses. "She's a bit of a wonder, you know," he said to the naval lieutenant who was his companion.

"It's a wild bird," the lieutenant agreed, and as the rest of the revue was merely frocks and the absence of frocks they went off to supper.

In the morning, which was Sunday, Birdie Bolton came to see Dr. Reginald Fortune. It was her remarkable creed that she could not live in a noise, and so for years she had owned a house in the still rural suburb of Westhampton where Reggie and his father practised. The elder Dr. Fortune at first looked after her, but when Reggie came on the scene Miss Bolton, declaring with her usual frankness that she liked her doctors young, turned herself over to him.

21

By daylight Miss Bolton dressed, and even overdressed, the part of a brisk British spinster. She was very tailor-made and severely tweedy, and thus looked leaner than ever. But her eyes retained a gleam of devilment.

"You gave us a great show last night," Reggie said.

"Were you in front?" said Miss Bolton, and made a face. "Oh, Lord! Sorry. I was rotten."

Reggie understood that his professional interest was required.

"What's the trouble?" he said cheerfully.

"That's your show," said Miss Bolton. "Put me through it."

The conversation then became confidential and dull upon the usual themes of a medical examination. At last, "Well, you know, we don't get to anything," Reggie said. "This is all quite good and normal. What's making you anxious?"

"Dreams," said Miss Bolton. "Why do I have dreams? I never dreamed in my life till now."

"What sort of dreams?"

"Oh, any old sort. Bally rot. One night it was a motor-bus chivvying me on the stage. One night May" — May Weston was her companion — "May would keep parrots in the bathroom. Then I hear a noise and wake up and there isn't any noise."

"Do you have this every night?"

"Snakes! Not much. Now and again. But I say, doc, it's not fair. I don't drink and I don't drug. But I'll be seeing pink rats if this goes on."

"Is there anything worrying you just now?"

Was it possible that Miss Bolton blushed? Reggie could not be sure. "You're a bright boy, doc. Be good!" She shook hands and gripped like a man. The big emerald she always wore ground into his fingers. "Birdie, the strong girl. Bye-bye," she laughed.

On the next morning Reggie was just out of his bath when he was told that Miss Bolton's housekeeper had rung up. Miss Bolton had had an accident and would he go at once. "Tell Sam," said Reggie, and jumped into his trousers. Samuel Baker, a young taxi-driver whose omniscient impudence had persuaded Reggie to enlist him as chauffeur and factotum, had the car round and some sandwiches inside it by the time Reggie was downstairs. Neither he nor Reggie lost time.

Normanhurst, Miss Bolton's house, stands by itself in an acre or so of garden, and is in the mid-Victorian or amorphous style. As Reggie jumped out of the car, the housekeeper opened the door. She was a brisk, buxom woman; she looked, and perhaps was, just what a housekeeper ought to be.

"What's wrong, Mrs. Betts?" Reggie said.

"It's very serious, sir. This way, please." She led the way to Birdie Bolton's boudoir, stopped, took a key from her apron pocket, and unlocked the door.

"Hallo!" Reggie said.

"I'm afraid you're going to have a shock, sir," said Mrs. Betts, and opened the door for him.

Reggie went in. The sunlight flooded Birdie Bolton's face, which was white. She lay on a sofa. She was in evening dress. There was an open wound in one side of her throat, and from it a red line lay across her bare shoulder, down her arm, to a purple stain on the carpet.

Reggie went across the room in two strides and bent over her. She had been dead for hours.

"Who found her, Mrs. Betts?"

"The upper housemaid, sir. She's been having hysterics ever since."

"Bah! Was the room just like this?"

"No, sir. Miss Weston was asleep in that chair."

"What?" Reggie stared. The mistress murdered and the companion placidly asleep by her side — perhaps that would not have startled his calm mind. But he knew May Weston, and had written her off as a dull, simple creature — a cushion of a girl.

"Miss Weston was asleep in that chair," the housekeeper repeated. "I saw her myself. I came in, sir, when Amelia — when the housemaid screamed. Miss Weston was in evening dress too. She didn't wake at the screaming either — just stirred. I went to her and shook her, and 'Miss Weston,' I said, 'whatever's this?' I said, and she woke up and looked round her, sort of heavy, and she saw Miss Bolton lying there and the blood, and she screamed out, 'I did it — oh, I did it,' and she looked at me very queer and she fainted." Mrs. Betts stopped and stared at Reggie, waiting for him to express horror.

"So what did you do with her?" said Reggie. Mrs. Betts swallowed. "I had her carried to her room. Dr. Fortune," she said with dignity. "I am told she's come to and been crying."

"Well, that's natural, anyway," said Reggie.

"Natural, indeed!" Mrs. Betts tossed her head.

"And what did you do next, Mrs. Betts?"

"I had nothing touched, sir. I locked up the room. And I telephoned to you and the police."

"I'm sure you behaved admirably, Mrs. Betts," Reggie murmured. Mrs. Betts was appeased. "I could hardly bear it, sir. Such a sweet, good mistress as she was. A perfect lady with all her little ways, as you know, sir. And that Miss Weston! So soft and quiet as she seemed. I don't mind saying, sir, I felt as if I was stone. Oh!" She shuddered and shook. "Vicious, I call it."

Reggie was looking round the room. "I suppose it is murder, sir?" said Mrs. Betts in a tone that suggested she would like to have the hanging of Miss Weston.

"I suppose it is," Reggie said. He crossed to the chair in which Miss Weston had been found sleeping and picked up from the floor close by a pair of scissors and a pointed bodkin with an ivory handle. Both were clotted with blood. Ugly things.

"Ah!" Mrs. Betts said. "That's what did it. Put 'em down, sir. I left them there by her chair for the police to see."

"You think of everything, Mrs. Betts," said Reggie, and put them down and went back to the body of Birdie Bolton.

That stab in the throat, it was "not so deep as a well, nor so wide as a church door"; it was a small wound to be mortal. A small neat wound which had rare luck to slit the jugular vein. Reggie looked back at the bodkin and the scissors. He noticed that Mrs. Betts had gone out.

There were other wounds. In half a dozen places the pallid shoulders and breast had bled. No one of these gashes was serious. They were just such as might be expected of those unhandy weapons, scissors and bodkin. It was that neat, lucky stroke at the throat which determined the fate of Birdie Bolton. The minor wounds suggested a struggle with someone in a passion, and that Miss Bolton had struggled Reggie found other evidence. The black evening dress had been dragged from one

24

shoulder and torn, and there on that right shoulder were the blue marks of a hand that had gripped. Reggie's examination became more minute.

Two men bustled in. A hand tapped Reggie's shoulder. "Now, sir, if you please."

Reggie stood up and confronted a pompous, portly little man.

"I am Dr. Fortune," Reggie said. "Miss Bolton was a patient of mine."

"Was," said the little man, with emphasis. "She is a case for an expert now, Dr. Fortune."

"That's why I was examining her," said Reggie sweetly.

The little man laughed. "A general practitioner is not much use to her now. Rather beyond you, isn't it?"

"Well, I've not made up my mind," Reggie said.

"Don't worry. Don't worry." He waved Reggie off, but Reggie did not go. "You'll only be in our way, you know. We'll let you know if we want you at the inquest. Just for formal evidence." Still Reggie did not move. "I am the divisional surgeon, sir," said the little man loudly.

"I was wondering who you were," Reggie murmured.

The little man swung round. "We'll have the room cleared, inspector," he said.

The detective inspector, who looked more like a policeman than seemed possible, strode heavily forward. "Hope you're not meaning to give trouble, doctor," he frowned. "Or I'll have to take steps."

"Fancy!" Reggie said. "Well, look where you're going." He walked across to the window and looked out at the roses.

"Clear out, please." The inspector followed him.

"Zeal, all zeal," Reggie murmured, and went.

There were two doors to the room. He did not use that by which they had come, but the other. He happened to know that it opened into Birdie Bolton's bedroom.

There was someone in the bedroom. A startled dark face peeped round the screen by the bed. It belonged to a smart lady's maid.

"Dear me, I thought this was the passage," Reggie said.

"It is Miss Bolton's bedroom — poor Miss Bolton." The maid had a slight foreign accent.

"Of course it is. And you're her maid, of course. Flora, isn't it?"

"Yes, sir. Yes, doctor. Ah, you have seen Miss Bolton! You cannot do anything—no?"

"Miss Bolton is dead, Flora."

"I was so fond of her," Flora sighed.

"Well, I liked her. I suppose you heard nothing last night?"

"Ah, no. She have sent me to bed. And I sleep so sound."

Reggie nodded. "It's a bad business, Flora. Take me to Miss Weston's room, will you?"

"Miss Weston! Ah!" Flora said, with tragic intensity.

"H'm. You think she——"

"I do not think. I feel," Flora said.

"It's a bad habit. Well——"

And Flora led the way. She was a plump woman of some age, but still comely enough in a dark, heavy fashion.

A tap at a door. "It is the doctor, Miss Weston," from Flora. A sullen voice, "You can come in," and in Reggie went.

May Weston was a squalid sight. Her natural prettiness, the prettiness of fresh youth, the bloom of pink and white, the grace of full, soft line had all gone from her. She lay a shapeless heap on her bed, her evening dress still on and all crushed and crumpled and awry, her yellow hair half down and tousled, her face of a bluish pallor.

"What do you want?" She stared at Reggie heavily.

"Well, this won't do, will it?" Reggie smiled cheerfully and sat down beside the bed. "So why are you like this?"

"Haven't you heard?" she cried.

"I've heard and seen," Reggie said. "I can't do any more there. But perhaps I can here." He began to feel her pulse.

"I'm not ill."

"Well, you never know." He let her wrist go and bent over her. "Sleep rather sound, don't you?"

"Oh!" She shuddered. "Why do you look at me like that?"

Reggie bent suddenly closer, and as suddenly sat up again. Then he laughed. "Like what, my dear?"

She stared at him and her lip quivered. "You—you! Oh, do you think I can be mad?"

Reggie shook his head. "Let's begin quite at the beginning. Let's preserve absolute calm. You dined with Miss Bolton last night alone? After dinner you went to her boudoir? That would be about nine?"

"Yes, yes. Mr. Ford came just after the coffee."

"Ah! And who is Mr. Ford?"

May Weston blushed abundantly. "We—he has been here a good deal," she stammered. "Oh, Dr. Fortune, it isn't his fault."

"Young or old, rich or poor—what is he?"

"Of course he's young. I suppose he's rich. His father makes engines or something in Leeds, and he is in the London office."

"Sounds solid," Reggie agreed. "And why does Mr. Ford call at nine p.m.?"

Miss Weston's blushes were renewed. "He has been very often," she said, and wrung her hands. "I shall have to tell, doctor, shan't I? Yes. He met Miss Bolton once at supper and then he used to come here."

"Ah! Good-looking fellow, is he?"

"Oh, yes. He is very big and handsome."

"And Miss Bolton liked him. Well, well." Reggie understood now why poor Birdie Bolton had been dreaming dreams of nights.

"Yes," said May Weston faintly. "Oh, it's a shame! But I must tell. She thought he came to see her, but— —"

"But it was really to see you. Now, let's get back to the coffee."

"He came last night. We were so gay. Miss Bolton—oh, poor Birdie!"

"We can't undo that, my dear. Let's do what we can for her. Did he stay late?"

"Rather. I don't know. I was sleepy. But Birdie was so gay. And then— and then he went away and Birdie began to talk about him. I don't know how it happened. She said something—and I felt I just had to tell her—I told her he had proposed to me. And then she was furious. Oh, have you ever seen her in one of her rages? She was terrible. She said dreadful things. And I—I felt as if I couldn't do anything at all. I was dazed and faint and just sat. I know she hit me."

"I saw the bruise," Reggie said gently, looking at the blue mark on her neck.

"Then she stormed out of the room, and—oh, doctor, I don't know— perhaps I fainted—it was as if I was all lead in that chair. I thought I was

27

asleep. And then it was like a horrible, horrible dream – I saw her being killed. She was on the sofa, and someone was hitting at her. Oh, doctor, did I do it? Was it a dream? Did I really do it?"

"You saw – or you dreamed – who was it struck her in your dream?"

"Oh, I don't know. It was just like a dream when you can't tell. I know it was Birdie. But was it me killed her?"

The door was flung open. The detective inspector strode in. "May Weston?" He was more the policeman than ever.

Reggie stood up. "How civil you are!" he said.

"You make yourself very busy, don't you?" The inspector glared. "Don't you interfere with me. May Weston – I shall charge you with the murder of your mistress, Birdie Bolton. Get up off that bed now."

"He's forgotten the rest of his part – 'anything you say may be used in evidence against you,' Miss Weston. So you'll say nothing, please."

The inspector grew red and puffed, and advanced upon Reggie. "Here, you – you clear out of this. You're obstructing me in – –"

"Is it possible?" Reggie drawled. "Well, it isn't necessary, anyway." and he left the inspector still swelling.

It is fair to him to add, what he has since protested, that he never liked May Weston. Pussy-cat is his name for her, and he is not fond of cats.

From her room he went to the telephone in the hall, and there the inspector, still rather flushed, found him again.

"And what might you be doing now, if you please?" said the inspector, with constabulary sarcasm.

"Oh, I'm talking to Miss Bolton's solicitors. Hadn't you thought of talking to Miss Bolton's solicitors?"

"Never you mind what I thought of. Don't you use that telephone again. I won't have it."

"Oh, yes, you will. Now I'm going to talk to Superintendent Bell." The inspector was visibly startled. For Superintendent Bell was near the summit of the Criminal Investigation Department. "Any objection? No? How nice of you. . . ." He conferred with the telephone, and at length: "Dr. Fortune. Yes. Oh, is that you, Bell? So glad. I wish you'd come along here, Normanhurst, Westhampton. One of my patients murdered. No, not by me. Quite unusual case. Yes, it is the Birdie Bolton case. The inspector in charge is such a good, kind man. Sweet face he has. You'll come right on?

So glad." Reggie put down the receiver and smiled upon the puzzled inspector. "That's that," he said, and went out. Samuel, the chauffeur, put away his picture paper. "I want my camera," Reggie said, and Samuel touched his hat and drove off. Reggie sauntered into the garden.

Normanhurst, as you know, is a low, spreading house of a comfortable Victorian dowdiness. There are — don't count the attics — only two storeys. It is old enough to be quite covered with climbing plants — ivy on the north, roses and a wisteria on the other sides. Birdie Bolton's bedroom and boudoir looked to the south, and were on the ground floor. On the north of the house is the approach from the high road, a curling drive through a shrubbery. Birdie Bolton's rooms looked out upon a rose-bed and a big lawn. About her windows climbed a big Gloire de Dijon. The roses beneath were of the newer hybrid teas, well cultivated, well chosen, and at their best — a fragrant pomp of red and gold. "How she loved 'em, poor soul," Reggie thought, and began to feel sentimental. That singular emotion was interrupted by the sound of a motor-car. He went back to the front of the house to meet it.

A big car was drawing up. It contained two people — a uniformed chauffeur and a large young man who jumped out, rather clumsily, before the car stopped. He had the good looks of a hero of musical comedy, but an expression rather sheepish than fatuous, and a pallid complexion.

"I think you are Mr. Ford." Reggie came close to him. "I am Dr. Fortune. Miss Bolton was a patient of mine. I hardly expected to see you so soon."

"Miss Weston sent for me, sir." Mr. Ford recoiled, for Reggie's face was very close to his.

"Did she, though!" Reggie murmured. "Did she really?" Miss Weston had forgotten to tell him that. Pussy-cat!

"Well, Flora telephoned for her. She said something terrible had happened, and Miss Weston wanted me. I say, doctor, what has happened?"

"Jolly kind of Flora," Reggie said. "Well, Mr. Ford, Miss Bolton has been murdered."

"My God!" said Mr. Ford, and became livid.

"And Miss Weston has been charged with the murder."

"Oh, my God!" Mr. Ford said again. "Oh, damn!" and put his hand to his head. "Here, let me go to her."

"I don't mind," said Reggie, and Mr. Ford plunged into the house.

Reggie remained on the steps waiting for fresh arrivals. The goggled chauffeur moved his car on out of the way, descended, and behind a laurustinus lit a cigarette. Reggie, who never smoked them, sniffed disapproval and began to fill a pipe.

A taxi-cab drove up, and out of it bounced a plump little man whose coat looked as if he wore stays.

"I am Dr. Fortune," Reggie said.

"And I'm Donald Gordon, doctor," said the little man, who was emphatically a Jew. "Moss and Gordon." It was the name of Miss Bolton's solicitors. "Many thanks for letting us know. Poor, dear Birdie. She was a peach. Let's have all the facts, please." He had an engaging lisp.

"There's a detective inspector inside. Like a bull in a china-shop."

"Had some," said Mr. Donald Gordon. "Come on, doctor. Hand it out."

"Well, let's see the flowers," Reggie said, and walked him into the garden and began to tell him all that he knew.

"So he's pinched Miss Weston, has he?" the little Jew lisped. "He's a hustler."

"Oh, I expect he's arrested Ford too, by now. Me and you in a minute. He's a zealous fellow. By the way, Gordon, who is Ford?"

"Yes. He's a dark horse, ain't he? I only met him once, doctor. You could see poor old Birdie was sweet on him."

"Oh, so Miss Weston was telling the truth about that."

"Why, didn't you believe her, doctor?"

"D'you know, I wonder if I believe anything I've heard in this house."

"Like that, is it?" Gordon lisped.

"Just like that," said Reggie. A gravity had come over the perky little Jew, which he found very engaging.

Mr. Gordon nodded at him. "Birdie was the one and only," he said, and Reggie nodded back.

"Nice flowers, doctor," a new voice said. Reggie turned to see the small insignificance of Superintendent Bell, greeted him heartily, and introduced Mr. Gordon. "Am I *de trop*, as the French say?" said Superintendent Bell. "No? Thought it might be a council of war."

"Oh, is it war?" Reggie said.

"Well, you know, you've quarrelled with Inspector Mordan." The Superintendent shook his head at Reggie.

"I wouldn't dare. He quarrelled with me."

"Such a pity." The Superintendent smiled and rubbed his hands. "I ought to tell you, doctor, I quite approve of everything that Inspector Mordan has done."

"Splendid force, the police," Mr. Gordon lisped. "Wonderful force. So forcible."

"Including the arrest of Miss Weston?" Reggie asked. "Well, well. Anyone else you'd like to arrest?"

"Any one you suggest, doctor? Now I ask you — what would you have done?"

"Oh, I'm not in the force."

"We do have to be so careful," the Superintendent sighed. "That's a handicap, that is. I wonder why you wanted me, doctor?"

"I'm frightened of your inspector. He's not chatty. I want to photograph the body."

The Superintendent turned to Gordon. "It's a taste, you know, that's what it is. He likes corpses. Speaking as man to man, doctor, are you working with us?"

"May I?"

"That's very handsome. Yes. Inspector Mordan, he has a kind of a manner, as you might say. I'll speak to him. Is there anything you'd like to tell me, doctor?"

"Nice flowers, aren't they?" Reggie nodded to the rose-bed under Birdie Bolton's window. It was minutely neat.

"Look as if they'd been brought up by hand," said the Superintendent, but he looked at Reggie, not the roses. "Anything queer, sir?"

"There's that," Reggie said. He pointed to a spray of the Gloire de Dijon beside the window. It bore a bud; it had been broken, and the bud was limp and dead.

"That wasn't broken last night," said the Superintendent.

"No. That's what's interesting," said Reggie, and turned away.

At the door and in the drive there was some congested traffic. Mr. Ford's big car still waited. Reggie's humbler car had come back with his

31

camera. The taxis of Mr. Gordon and Superintendent Bell took up more room. And yet another taxi was trying to get to the steps.

"Who's this, Superintendent?"

"I dare say it'll be for Miss Weston."

"Taking her to Holloway at once? Well, well. I dare say it's all for the best."

But Miss Weston was not to go without a noise. Mr. Ford saw to that. At the head of the stairs he conducted an altercation with Inspector Mordan in which defiance, abuse, and profane swearing were his chief arguments. It was beastly stupid and it was damned impudence to arrest Miss Weston, and it was also beastly impudence and damned stupid, and so forth. In the midst of which the wretched girl was shepherded by two detectives downstairs.

"My God, you might as well arrest me!" Mr. Ford cried, in final desperation.

"Perhaps I will," said the Inspector heavily, and glowered at him.

Mr. Ford paled and drew back.

On the stairs below Miss Weston stopped and turned. "Oh, Edmund, don't," she said. "They can't hurt me. You know they can't."

Superintendent Bell drew Reggie aside.

"Think that throws any light?" Reggie said.

"Well, not a searchlight," said the Superintendent.

Miss Weston was driven off. Mr. Ford, looking dazed, came slowly downstairs, and to him went Gordon.

"Better get her a solicitor, you know," Gordon said.

"By Jove, that's it!" Mr. Ford cried, and plunged out.

The Inspector and the Superintendent exchanged glances and looked at Gordon.

"Why did you put him on to that, sir?" said the Superintendent.

"Professional feeling, dear boy," Gordon smiled. "Nice girl, ain't it? I fancy my firm are Miss Bolton's executors, and I fancy that bird is sole legatee."

The Superintendent pursed his lips. The Inspector laughed. "It grows, don't it, sir? Just grows," he said.

"I would like to get on," Reggie yawned.

"That's right," said the Superintendent, and took the Inspector aside.

Mr. Gordon, following Reggie to the boudoir, was distressed by the sight of the dead body, and said so. Reggie went on with his photography — first the stab in the throat, then the minor wounds, then the bruise on the shoulder. At which last Inspector Mordan found him.

"Taking the wrong side, aren't you?" he sneered.

"Oh, I'm taking all sides. Ever try it?" Reggie said.

"Well, have you done, doctor?" the little Jew broke in. "Can't we have her covered up?"

"I'll have the body removed, sir. If the doctor has quite done." said the Inspector.

And so at last the body of Birdie Bolton was taken away to the mortuary, and Mr. Gordon, much relieved, flung open the windows and turned to his business, the secretaire and its papers. He worked quickly. . . . "Nothing there but love-letters. Wonder where she kept her will?"

"There's a safe in the bedroom, I think," Reggie said.

"You bet there is. She had all her jewels in the house, I know, and she had some good stuff, poor old girl. Well, come on; here's her keys."

They went into the bedroom, and the little Jew made for the safe. Reggie wandered across the room. It was a parquet floor with Persian rugs on it. He shifted one by the bedside. There was a small dark stain on the floor still not dry. An exclamation from Gordon made him turn. Gordon had the safe open, and the safe, but for some papers in disorder, was empty.

"Not one bally bangle left!" Gordon cried. "Not a sparkle of the whole outfit! Remember that ruby and diamond breastplate! Remember her pearls! And the stuff that Indian Johnny gave her! My hat! Somebody's had a haul." A spasm crossed his face. "I say, doctor, you were here when I opened the safe!"

"I was here," Reggie said stolidly. "I wasn't surprised." The little Jew gasped. "You remember that emerald she always wore? It wasn't on the dead body."

"Oh, God!" said Gordon, and with unsteady hands turned over the papers. "That's her script. More or less all there, I should say. Where's the will? I know she had her will. Drew it myself."

"What's that?" Reggie said.

33

The one untidy thing in that very tidy room, a paper lay by the fireplace. Gordon picked it up. "Here we are! Yes, 'May Grace Weston, my companion.' That's the document. Crumpled up and torn!" He whistled. "As if Birdie was destroying it and then—biff!"

"Just as if she'd been destroying it," Reggie agreed.

"That puts the lid on, don't it!" said the little Jew. "Miss Weston-oh, lor, there's a soft kid if you ever had one. Just shows you you never know with girls, doctor. Girls, girls, girls! Well, we'd better tell these bally policemen."

So Inspector Mordan, vastly to his satisfaction, was told, and Superintendent Bell, appearing from nowhere, heard, and agreed to search the house for the stolen jewels. "You gentlemen come too, please." He cocked an eye at Reggie.

"Want to keep me under observation?" Reggie grinned back.

"Want you to identify what we find," said the Inspector.

"You'll find something all right," said Reggie.

But he showed little interest in the search, mooning after their men in and out of servants' bedrooms and yawning in corners. Inspector Mordan had gone straight to Miss Weston's room, and from it he came glowing with triumph. He called for his Superintendent, he collected Reggie and Gordon. "You gentlemen happen to recognize that?" He opened his big hand and showed the ring with the big emerald which Birdie Bolton had loved.

"That's it," Gordon cried. "That's Birdie's. Coo! What a stone, ain't it?"

"In Weston's room," the Inspector proclaimed, "on the floor; just under the bed, in Weston's room."

"Only that and nothing more?" Reggie murmured.

"Yes, where's the rest, Mordan?" said Superintendent Bell.

The Inspector smote his thigh. "By George, I see it! I let that rascal Ford see the wench alone. He's gone off stuffed with the swag."

"That's a thought," Reggie admitted, and the Superintendent lifted an eyebrow at him. "You ought to have Ford watched. No, I mean it. If I was you, Inspector, I'd have his place watched night and day."

The Inspector was visibly gratified. "I know my business, thank you," he said. "I say, doctor—it is growing, isn't it?"

"Oh, yes, as if it was forced," Reggie smiled.

34

"What do you mean?" The Inspector flushed.

"You see, you're so witty, Mordan," said the Superintendent.

"And that's that," Reggie yawned. "You don't really want me anymore. Good-bye. Oh, Inspector—I don't want you to be disappointed. The murder wasn't done in that room where you found the body. Good-bye!"

"Wasn't done——" The Inspector stared after him. "Good Lord, he's mad!"

"Better get him to bite you, Mordan," said the Superintendent.

*　　*　　*　　*　　*　　*

That party did not meet again till the day of the inquest. Before the court met, Superintendent Bell called on Reggie and found him in a bad temper. This was unusual, and equally unusual in the Superintendent's experience was a pallor, a certain tension, across Reggie's solid, amiable face. A civil question about his health brought a snappish answer. It seemed to the Superintendent that Dr. Fortune had been making a night of it.

"Well, what is it?" Reggie snarled. "Got anything to tell me?"

"I've been rather disappointed," the Superintendent said meekly.

"More fool you. I told you to watch Ford."

"That's it, sir. Were you pulling my leg?"

"Oh, damn it, man, this is serious! Miss Bolton was a patient of mine. I don't let anyone but me kill my patients."

"Very proper, I'm sure," the Superintendent agreed. "But we have watched him, doctor. Nothing doing."

"Set a man to stand on his doorstep, I suppose. What's the good of that?"

"As you say," the Superintendent agreed. "We've picked up one thing, though. Just before the murder his father turned him down for wanting to marry this girl Weston. He hasn't a penny except from his father. That might have made him desperate—him and the girl. It does grow, you know, doctor."

"Queer case," Reggie grunted. "Going to the inquest? Sorry I can't drive you down. My chauffeur's taking a day off."

So they walked to the coroner's court, and on the way Superintendent Bell used his large experience in the art of extracting confidences in vain.

But Reggie mellowed, perceptibly mellowed, as he baffled Superintendent Bell.

The court was crowded to its last inch. The coroner was conscious of his importance, and made the most of it in a long harangue. The divisional surgeon was more pompous than ever, and made it a point of honour to use terms so technical that all his evidence had to be translated to the jury, and the coroner and he argued over the translation.

"What a life, ain't it?" Mr. Gordon murmured in Reggie's ear.

At last came what the evening papers called "Dramatic Evidence": the housemaid who had found the body and had hysterics over again as she described it; Mrs. Betts, who had found May Weston sleeping beside it, waked her, and heard her say, "I did it — oh, I did it!"

"Sensation in Court" was the cross-head for that. The coroner looked over his glasses at the jury, and the jury muttered together, and May Weston came into the box. With the manner of a chaplain at an execution the coroner warned her that she need not give answers that would incriminate her. "I want to tell you everything," she said. She was very pale in her black, and listless of manner, but quite calm.

What she told was the queer story she had told Reggie, but she was not allowed to tell it her own way. The coroner badgered her with continual questions designed to make the queerness of it seem queerer. He made her nervous, confused her, and frightened her. "You bother me so that I don't know if I'm telling the truth or not," she quavered.

Then, in the language of the newspapers, "another sensation." Mr. Ford, large and red, started up and roared, "I ought to be there, sir. Let her alone. I ought to be there."

Reggie put his head between his hands and bowed himself, groaning.

Everyone else was much excited by Mr. Ford. He was pulled down in his seat. The coroner rebuked him with awful majesty. The foreman of the jury wanted to know if he would be called. The coroner pronounced that the court would most certainly require Mr. Ford to explain himself — and came back to May Weston.

"The fool that he is, he's done the trick, though," Reggie muttered to Mr. Gordon, and Gordon nodded and grinned. For after this interruption the coroner handled May Weston much more gently, almost indulgently, as a good man sorry for a woman's weakness. And he was soon done with her.

"Any questions?" He looked at the lawyers. Reggie bent forward and whispered to the solicitor appearing for Miss Weston.

That large, bland man stood up. "Now, Miss Weston, about that coffee." He had his reward. Everyone in the court, and Miss Weston not least, stared surprise at him. Slowly he extracted from her (she seemed bewildered at each question) the whole history of that after-dinner coffee. Coffee had been brought to the boudoir just before Mr. Ford came; no one but she had expected Mr. Ford; another cup was brought for Mr. Ford; Mr. Ford and she had both drunk their coffee. Miss Bolton — why, no, Miss Bolton had not. Miss Bolton had been very gay, and in doing a few steps of a dance had upset her coffee.

"No more questions, sir." The large solicitor sat down smiling.

The coroner was visibly unable to understand him, and made a great business with his papers. It was now long after tea-time. "I suppose we shan't finish to-day, gentlemen?" the coroner suggested.

"Quite impossible, sir," said the large solicitor cheerfully. "I have some long medical evidence. Dr. Fortune, Miss Bolton's physician. The first medical man who saw the lady. The first medical man who saw Miss Weston."

The court rose. Reggie, with Gordon at his heels, went out by the solicitor's door and found Superintendent Bell waiting for him. "Now are you playing the game, doctor?" said Superintendent Bell sadly.

"For keeps," Reggie laughed. "Come and dine with me. Bring Mordan. He's so genial."

"We do have to take these little things so seriously," the Superintendent murmured.

But a party of four, the Superintendent and the large Inspector, Reggie and the little Jew, packed themselves into a taxi-cab and drove into town. Reggie was full of elegant conversation. He grew iris, and told them all about iris, with appendices on the costumes in revue.

Once or twice Superintendent Bell tried to turn his attention to serious subjects. Vainly. At last Inspector Mordan broke out with, "I say, doctor, what's the wheeze about the coffee?"

"The Inspector touches the spot. Care not, all will be known ere long. There's a jolly little iris from the Himalayas ‒ ‒ " Reggie returned with enthusiasm to horticulture.

"Where are you taking us, doctor?" said the Superintendent. The taxi, which had for some little time been running through the city, seemed to intend coming out on the other side — a locality promising no good dinner. As he spoke, it turned into Liverpool Street Station.

"Liverpool Street, by George!" the Inspector said. "This is a bean-feast. Going to take us to Epping Forest, doctor?"

"We may have to go farther," Reggie said, and Gordon laughed.

"Are you in this, sir?" The Inspector turned on him.

"Professional secret, dear boy."

Reggie led the way to the station dining-room. "I don't know the cook. But let's hope for the best. A tirin' day, an active evening. Strength is what we need. Strength without somnolence. Salmon, I see. Lamb chops, I would add. One of your younger ducks would comfort me. Do you sleep after Burgundy, Inspector? A warm night, as you say. Larose is a genial claret. Let us all be genial."

"Well, you're a bit supercilious," the Inspector complained.

"How can you say so? I am keeping all the glory for you. Glory on ice. All ready for Inspector Mordan. So gather you roses while you may. Talking of roses, what do you think of the hybrid Austrian briers?" He explained what he thought of them to a silent audience, sliding gracefully into an appreciation of salmon eaten at Waterford, at Exeter, and at Berwick. Few are the men who will not talk about food. The detectives produced much valuable experience of bourgeois cookery, and the dinner went merrily. In its later stages Reggie became silent and watched the clock. He seemed to grudge Inspector Mordan his cheese, and as soon as it was swallowed made a move.

"Well, doctor, I did think we should have had some coffee," the Inspector chuckled.

But Reggie was already making for the door. By the door stood his chauffeur looking for him. Reggie beckoned impatiently to the detectives and followed the chauffeur out. He led them to the main line departure platforms. It was near the time of the Harwich boat-train. A dark, wiry man was registering some luggage for Amsterdam. By his side stood a veiled woman of full figure. Both he and she carried suit-cases. As the man turned round he bumped into Reggie, who was looking the other way, and seemed to have some difficulty in disentangling himself. He glared at Reggie and hurried away. The woman was ahead of him.

Reggie grabbed Superintendent Bell. "See that pair. Take them both. Picking my pocket. Get the bags."

Bell and Mordan hurried after the pair. Bell tapped the man's shoulder, and he jumped round.

"I thought so. You'll come with me to the station, my man," said Superintendent Bell, with admirable calm.

"What is it?" the man cried. His accent was slightly foreign. "What station? What do you mean?"

"You know all right," said the Superintendent. "I am Superintendent Bell of Scotland Yard."

"I do not know at all," the man protested. "What do you want with me?"

The woman saw Reggie. She hissed something to the man in a foreign argot, and turned to run. The Superintendent laid hold of her. Inspector Mordan closed with the man. The Inspector was large and brawny, but at the end of a moment he was on his back and the man making off. Reggie dived for his legs in the manner of Rugby football, and they went down together.

The railway police came on the scene. The man was handcuffed, and he and the woman and the two detectives packed into a cab. Reggie and Gordon followed in another to the police station in Old Jewry.

When they arrived, the two prisoners were already in the charge-room and the woman was protesting vehemently, to the great edification of the uniformed inspector at the desk and a plain-clothes friend of his, and the embarrassment of Superintendent Bell and Inspector Mordan. It was an outrage. Why did they assault her and her husband? Why? They were respectable people. She would not endure it.

"Oh, Flora, Flora!" Reggie shook his head at her.

The woman whirled round on him. "You! Ah, it is you, then, the doctor. You are a traitor. You are a wicked villain. I spit upon you." And she did. The man said something to her in the strange foreign argot they seemed to use between themselves, and she was silent.

The plain-clothes man came forward grinning. "Why, Bunco! It is my dear old pal, Bunco! What have they got you for now, old thing?" The man scowled. Dusty and bruised from the scuffle and in the ignominy of handcuffs, he had still a certain arrogant dignity. He was well made for all his slightness, and the strength which had upset Mordan showed in his poise. It was a dark, aquiline face with a good brow, but passionate and cruel.

"What is the charge, doctor?" said Superintendent Bell.

"Oh. On the seventh instant—murder of Wilhelmina, otherwise Birdie Bolton," Reggie drawled. "Better search them."

"It is a lie!" Flora screamed; and continued to scream.

Reggie and Gordon were smoking in another room when Bell and Mordan came back with the results of the search. A suit-case was put on the table, opened, and seemed to be full of light, a mass of jewels.

"Can you identify, gentlemen?" Mordan said.

Superintendent Bell laid on the table a sheath knife. An unusual knife, rather long, rather narrow, rather stiff. "I'll identify that," Reggie said, and took it up. "That's the thing that killed her!"

"Coo!" said Mr. Gordon. "You've got a real head, doctor. This is Birdie's bunch all right. Swear to those rubies anywhere."

"Who's the man?" said Reggie.

Superintendent Bell sat down with a bump. "He asks me that." He appealed to the company. "I put it to you. He asks me that! The woman—she's Miss Bolton's maid, of course. But the man——"

"Oh, he's Ford's chauffeur. I told you to watch Ford. But you only sat on the steps of his flat. You've given me a lot of trouble, you know. I was up all last night. Chauffeur doesn't sleep in, of course. But who is he?"

"We call him Bunco in the Force," said the Superintendent meekly. "He's a jewel thief. Quite in the front of the profession. American-Austrian, I think. I believe Nastitch is his name—Alexander Nastitch or Supilo."

"Croat, I think," Reggie said. "This knife—they use 'em down that way."

"Coo! Tell us something you don't know," said the little Jew.

Reggie laughed. You may have noticed that he had his vanities. He passed his cigar-case round. "Where will I begin?" said he.

"At the beginning, please." Mordan grinned.

"The Inspector touches the spot as ever. Well, it hasn't been quite fair. I had the start of you. On the day before the murder Birdie Bolton consulted me. She hadn't been sleeping well. Heard noises at night. Now you see your way, don't you? No? Dear, dear. And I showed you that broken rose! Well, well. These two beauties, Flora and Nastitch, I suppose they got their situations to have a go for the jewels. Nastitch, as Ford's chauffeur, would have an excuse for hanging round the house and a car to use. He's had the car out of the garage till the small hours several times. I think he got in by the window last week — more than once, perhaps. And each time poor Birdie stirred. Better for her if she hadn't, poor girl. But they didn't mean murder, bless 'em. So they chose to drug her. There was morphia in that coffee. As you heard to-day, Birdie didn't drink hers. Another rotten chance. So May Weston went to sleep while Birdie was storming at her. Birdie raged off to her room. Whether she got out that will and tore it, we'll never know. It may have been Flora's little game. Nastitch came in, reckoning she was sure to be sound, and Flora was with him, I think. Birdie was very wide awake. There was a struggle and he stabbed her. He's a hot-tempered devil, as you saw to-day."

"This is all very pretty, doctor, but it ain't all evidence," Mordan said.

"You're so hasty. When she was dead, they took her into the boudoir where the Weston girl was asleep. They laid her on the couch and stabbed at her with her scissors and the bodkin. Filthy trick. That was what May Weston saw in the opium dream. Then I suppose they cleared the safe, and Nastitch went off. Flora annexed the emerald ring. Her perquisite, I suppose. Now, you shall have your evidence. When I came to the body, I saw those scissors never did the business. Ever tried killing anybody with scissors, Inspector? Poor game. No. We wanted something like this." He fingered the knife affectionately. "Just like this. Also somebody had left his mark on Birdie — a queer hand — a hand that wasn't quite all there — long fingers with no top joint. Did you notice Mr. Nastitch's left hand?"

The detectives looked at each other.

"That was in a burglary in New York," said the Superintendent. "He escaped out of a window, and a constable smashed his hand on the sill."

"So I photographed the wound and the bruise. Well, when I saw Weston, I saw she had really been drugged. Contracted pupils, bluish pallor. Morphia. Same symptoms in Ford. Why should they drug themselves and not drug Birdie? That ruled them out. Also, I surprised Flora in Birdie's bedroom doing something by the bed. When I browsed round afterwards I found a wet bloodstain under a clean rug. When Flora knew the Weston girl was arrested and the jewels had been missed, she chucked the ring into Weston's room. While you were searching the house, I drifted into Miss Flora's room. Several medicine bottles about. One of 'em empty. That had carried a strong solution of morphia. So I set my chauffeur to watch for Flora. And that night she went off to the lodgings of Nastitch. She's been buzzing round ever since. Well?"

"Well, sir, it's a good thing you didn't take to crime," said Superintendent Bell.

"Oh, that's much harder," said Reggie.

CASE III:
THE NICE GIRL

SOME are born great, some achieve greatness, and some have greatness thrust upon them. That was Dr. Reginald Fortune's trouble. He had become a specialist, and, as he told anybody who would listen, thought it an absurd thing to be. For he was interested in everything, but not in anything in particular. And it was just this various versatility of mind and taste which had condemned him to be a specialist. Obviously an absurd world.

The Criminal Investigation Department, solicitors, and others dealing with those experiments in social reform which are called crimes, by continually appealing to his multifarious knowledge and his all-observant eye, turned Dr. Reginald Fortune, general practitioner at Westhampton, into Mr. Fortune of Wimpole Street, specialist in — what shall we say? — the surgery of crime. And Reggie Fortune, though richer for the change, was not grateful. He liked ordinary things, and any day would have gladly bartered a murder for a case of chicken-pox. This accounts for his unequalled sanity of judgement.

Reggie was in that one of his clubs which he liked best, because no member of it knew anything about his profession. He had just completed an animated discussion on the prehistoric art of the French Congo, and was going out, when the tape machine buzzed and clicked at his elbow, and he stopped to look.

"Murder of Sir Albert Lunt," said the tape and, "Oh, my aunt!" said Reggie. The tape continued the conversation — thus: "Sir Albert Lunt, the well-known mining magnate, was found dead this afternoon in the deer park of his estate at Prior's Colney, Bucks. The body was discovered by an employee, in circumstances which suggested foul play. A medical examination led to the conclusion that the deceased had been shot. The local police have the case in hand, and search is being actively prosecuted for — —" Words failed the tape, and it relapsed into a buzz.

Reggie stared at it with gloomy apprehension. "I believe the beggars get murdered just to bother me," he was reflecting, when a jovial tea-merchant (wholesale — that club is a most respectable club) clapped him on the shoulder, and asked what the news was. "They only do it to annoy because they know it teases," said Reggie, and held up the tape.

"Albert Lunt!" said the tea-merchant, and whistled. "Well, he won't be missed!"

"Don't you believe it," Reggie groaned, and went out.

Upon his way home the passionate interest which the world, expressing its emotions on newspaper placards, took in Sir Albert Lunt was heaped upon him. When he let himself in, his factotum, Samuel Baker, was hovering in the hall.

"Oh, don't look so alert, Sam. It's maddening," Reggie complained.

Samuel Baker grinned. "You'll want all the papers, sir?"

"I suppose so!"

"I'm getting each edition as they come along, sir. Would you like a photograph of Sir Albert?"

"Go away, Sam." Reggie waved at him. "Go quite away, Sam. Do you know one reason why many fellows get murdered? It's because other fellows can't live up to them."

As he changed, Reggie looked through the papers. They were eloquent upon Sir Albert Lunt. His career, even when treated with the delicacy due to those who die rich, was a picturesque subject. Sir Albert Lunt, with his surviving brother Victor, had gone out to South Africa in the early days of diamonds. His first vocation was discreetly veiled. Some references to his life-long passion for sport reminded the knowing of the story that he and his brother had been in the front rank of the profession which works with three cards, the thimble, and the pea. Sir Albert, always in close alliance with Victor, had come out into daylight in the second stage of the diamond fields, when the business man was following in the steps of lucky adventurers. It had been Sir Albert's habit through life to appear in the second stage of things. The polite newspaper biographies called this prudence and sound judgment. He had always been fortunate in reaping other people's harvests. There were strange tales of his devices at Kimberley and Johannesburg, and just a hint of a clash with Cecil Rhodes, in which Rhodes had said what he thought of the Brothers Lunt with a certain gusto.

So ways that were dark and tricks that were anything but vain in Kimberley and Johannesburg made Albert Lunt a millionaire. He was not satisfied. South Africa was too small for him. Or was it too hot for him? He had spread his "operations" round the world. He was "interested" in some Manchurian tin and the copper belt of the Belgian Congo. "One of our modern Empire builders," as the evening papers sagely said.

How Sir Albert came by his title was a problem left in decent obscurity. Much was said of the magnificence of his life in England, his rococo palace not quite in Park Lane, his pantomime splendours at Prior's Colney — the ball-room which was in the lake, and the dining-room which was panelled in silver. The knowing reader could divine that Sir Albert had lived not only blatantly but hard and fast.

"Yah," said Reggie Fortune.

Just as he was putting on his coat, Sam arrived with a photograph of Sir Albert, and Reggie sat down to it. A plump man of middle height, rather loudly dressed; a long, heavy face, rather like a horse's, but with protruding eyes — commonplace enough. It was only the expression which made Reggie examine the fellow more closely. Under the photographic smirk was a look of insolence and conceit of singular force. The man who owned that would never allow any creature a right against him. Behold the secret of Sir Albert Lunt's success. And "Oh, Peter, I don't wonder someone murdered the animal," said Reggie. "Justifiable porcicide."

On which he went off to dinner with his sister, who had married a man in the Treasury, and gave him the pleasant somnolent evening you would expect.

When he came back there were two telegrams waiting for him.

Number one: "Was called in to Lunt case. Desire consult you. Lady Lunt also anxious your opinion. — GERALD BARNES."

Number two: "Desire consult you Lunt case. Please see me Prior's Colney morning. — LOMAS."

Reggie whistled. "Let 'em all come," said he.

Gerald Barnes had been house surgeon when Reggie was surgical registrar at St. Simon's Hospital, and had gone into practice somewhere in

Buckinghamshire. The Hon. Stanley Lomas was the head of the Criminal Investigation Department.

"Have they had a scrap?" Reggie smiled to himself. "Lots of zeal at Prior's Colney. Sam! The car after breakfast. We'll go and see life." And he went to bed.

But in the morning, just as he was finishing breakfast, he was told that Nurse Dauntsey wanted to see him and said it was most urgent. Nurse Dauntsey was at St. Simon's Hospital and had a partiality for Reggie, who (quite paternally) liked her for being gentle and kindly and pretty. A trim figure, a pair of honest grey eyes, a wholesome complexion, and an engaging red mouth were the best of Nurse Dauntsey's charms, but there was a simplicity about her which commended them. "Types of English Beauty. — Third Prize, Nurse Dauntsey," somebody said once. And it was felt to be just.

On this morning Nurse Dauntsey's nice face was troubled, and she had lost her usual calm. "Oh, Mr. Fortune, will you help me?" She rushed at Reggie. "It's the Lunt case."

"Now what in wonder have you to do with the Lunt case?"

Nurse Dauntsey blushed. "I'm engaged, Mr. Fortune," she said.

"Well, he's a very lucky man. And I hope you're a lucky girl."

"Oh, I am," said Nurse Dauntsey, with conviction. "He has been arrested. They say he murdered Sir Albert Lunt. Mr. Fortune, you will help us?"

"Who in creation is the lucky man?"

"His name is Vernon Cranford. He's a mining engineer. Oh, he's been everywhere. He's a born explorer, you know. He discovered a copper mine in Portuguese East Africa, one of the richest mines in the world. He came home last year and told Sir Albert Lunt about it, and Sir Albert sent him out to show the place. There was a sort of expedition, you know. And then, somehow, on the way up country Vernon was left behind. The other men tricked him. And when he got back to Mozambique he found that the other men had claimed the place was theirs. They had — what do you call it? — secured the concession, the rights in it. Wasn't it a shame? Vernon was just furious. I don't know quite how it happened. He only came back on Monday. I know he thought it was Sir Albert Lunt's fault. He said he was going to see him and have it out with him. He was going to see him yesterday. And then, last night, I had this note from him." She held it out, then couldn't bear to let it out of her hands, and so read it to him.

"'DEAR JO, — you mustn't worry. Lunt's been found shot, and the police have pinched me. Take it easy and go slow, and we'll comb it all out. — Yours, V.'"

Nurse Dauntsey gazed at Reggie with very big eyes.

"Sounds as if he knew his own mind," Reggie murmured. "And all this bein' thus, you want me to take up the case. Why?"

Nurse Dauntsey was startled. "But to get him off, of course — to defend him."

"Yes. But don't let's be previous. Speakin' frankly, did he do it?"

Nurse Dauntsey stood up. "I am engaged to him, Mr. Fortune," she said with dignity.

"Quite. That's the best thing I know about him. But I don't know much else."

"And I am sure he's not guilty."

"That kind of man, is he?"

"Just that kind of man," said Nurse Dauntsey, and her eyes glowed. "He couldn't do anything that wasn't fair and clean."

"Then he'd better have a solicitor. Do you suppose he's got one?"

"He'd never think of such a thing."

"Make him have Moss and Gordon. Ask for Donald Gordon, and say I sent you."

"But I want you, Mr. Fortune. You know there's no one like you."

"I blush. We both blush." Reggie smiled at her. "Well, nurse, two other people have called me into the Lunt case." Nurse Dauntsey cried out, and her nice face was piteous. "Take it easy and go slow, as V. Cranford says. I'm going down to Prior's Colney now to find out who I'm acting for. Oh, my dear girl, don't cry. I'm guessing it may be you. Now you be a good girl, and take Donald Gordon to him."

Nurse Dauntsey held out her hands. "Oh, Mr. Fortune, don't go against him," she cried.

Safe in his car, Reggie communed with himself. "She's a lamb. But disturbing to the intellects. Well, well. I'll have to make Brer Lomas sit up and take notice."

47

It was a clear cold morning of early spring, and Reggie shrank under his rugs. He had no love for east winds. He thought that there should be a close time for murders. He was elaborating a scheme by which the murder and the cricket seasons should be conterminous, when, at about twenty-five miles from London, they passed a horrible building. It was some distance from the high road, perched on the top of a small hill. It was of very red brick and very white stone, so arranged as to suggest the streaky bacon which might be made of a pig who had died in convulsions. It was ornate with the most improbable decorations, colonnades, battlements, a spire or so, oriel windows, a dome, Tudor chimneys, and some wedding-cake furbelows.

Reggie writhed and called to his factotum, who was sitting beside the chauffeur. "Sam, who had that nightmare?"

"That must be Colney Towers, sir. Mr. Victor Lunt's place."

Reggie groaned. "And Victor yet lives!"

A mile or two farther on they ran into a village which, before ruthless fellows stuck garden-city cottages on to it, must have been placid and pretty. The car drew up at an honest Georgian lump of red brick which bore the plate of Dr. Gerald Barnes.

Gerald Barnes was a ruddy young man who looked and dressed like a farmer. "I say, this is very decent of you. Jolly day, isn't it?" he bustled.

"Have you a fire, Barnes — a large fire? Put me on it," said Reggie. "And don't be so cheerful. It unnerves me." Still in his fur coat, Reggie planted himself in front of the consulting-room hearth. "Now, what do you want me for?"

"Well, it's not so much me, though I'd like your opinion. It's more Lady Lunt. Medically speaking, it's a pretty straight case. Lunt was shot in the chest and the bullet lodged in the spine, .38 revolver bullet. So there's not much doubt about the cause of death, what? But there are one or two odd things. The right thumb seems to be sprained. There's a nasty wound over the left eye — seems to have been made by a blow."

"Sounds messy. Where do I come in?"

"Why, I don't quite see my way through it. If a fellow had a pistol ready to use, why bash the beggar? It's a futile sort of wound too, nasty mess, but not dangerous. But you'd better see the body. Fortune."

"Oh, let me thaw. So Lady Lunt's not satisfied with the police?"

48

"No, by Jove, she isn't. I say, Fortune, how did you know that?"

"Genius, just genius. And what's Lady Lunt like?"

"Well, you know, she isn't quite a lady. And yet she is in big things. He married her about ten years ago, somewhere on the Continent. But she's English. She was a dancer or singer or something. Pretty low class, I believe. She was awfully handsome — big, dark, dashing type. She hasn't kept her looks, but she's still striking. She was pretty rowdy at first — went the pace like he did. He was an awful old bounder, you know. But for a good while now she's been different — quiet and serious — looking after things down here, good work on the estate — that sort of thing. She quietened him down too, but he was pretty bad. I think she was getting him in hand slowly, but she must have been having a rotten time for years."

"And what does Lady Lunt want now?"

"I'm hanged if I know," said Barnes, after some hesitation. "She thinks there's more in it than the detectives see, and she's not satisfied about this arrest."

"Now go easy. Two other people have called me in, and I don't know who I'll act for. So don't spoil anybody's game. Lomas wired for me — — "

"Lomas! So Scotland Yard isn't so mighty cocksure."

"Did Lomas seem so? Rude fellow. And then there's V. Cranford."

"Cranford's got to you already! He's lost no time."

"Oh, he's in very good hands. Now let's take a walk. You'll show me where Lunt was killed, and I'll have a look at him." Reggie shed his fur coat and became brisk.

It was his bailiff who had found Sir Albert Lunt, taken the news to the house, and telephoned for Gerald Barnes. Sir Albert Lunt had been walking back from his home farm across the park, which was an undulating stretch of turf over chalk, broken here and there by some fine beeches and coverts of gorse and bramble. A gravel path ran straight from the home farm to the main chestnut avenue. Barnes halted at a place where the turf was trampled in half-frozen footprints. Reggie looked round him. "Humph! Well out of sight of any house. Nobody heard the shot?"

"Nobody noticed it. It's a good way from the house, you see, and a mile from the farm. A shot or so — what's that in the open country? You often hear a gun somewhere."

"Quite. Where's that path go to?" Reggie pointed to a track across the turf diverging from the gravel.

"That? Oh, over to Victor Lunt's place. His park—he calls it a park too, but it's a small affair—almost joins this, you know."

"Well, well, let's see the body," Reggie yawned, and they marched on to Prior's Colney.

It had once been a comely place in a staid eighteenth-century fashion. "Oh, my only aunt!" Reggie groaned. "Looks like your grandmother put into the Russian ballet." It was loaded with excrescences of contorted ornament still raw and new against the mellow solemnity of the original homely house.

A motor-car stood at the door. While they were detaching hats and sticks in the hall, they could hear someone being told that Lady Lunt was not leaving her room. Then, being shown out, came a bulky man muffled in a fur coat with a big Astrakhan collar. He had a large head and a long face of unhealthy complexion. Across the forehead from right eyebrow to hair was a red furrow. He had prominent, pale eyes.

"Who is the sportsman with the scratched face?" Reggie said, as the door shut on him.

"Oh, that's Victor Lunt. Been inquiring after Lady Lunt, I suppose."

"Bright and brotherly," Reggie murmured.

There appeared briskly a man of grave and military aspect, who was presented to Reggie as Radnor Hall, Sir Albert Lunt's secretary. Radnor Hall (in a faintly American accent) was very glad to see Mr. Fortune; hoped for Mr. Fortune's company to lunch; after which, Lady Lunt was most anxious to see Mr. Fortune.

"I want to see the body," Reggie said gruffly.

So to the body he was taken, and saw that Gerald Barnes was right enough: there could be no doubt of the cause of death. A pistol bullet, fired from some little distance, had entered the chest and lodged in the spinal vertebræ. Sir Albert Lunt might not have died on the instant. He could not have lived long. But that mortal wound was tiny. What made the dead man look horrible was the gash in his forehead and the bruise round it. And over that Reggie frowned and pondered. "Showy, isn't it, very showy?" he complained. Such a hurt a man might get by falling on a stone. But Sir Albert Lunt had fallen on his back on the turf. If someone had hit him with a stone or some such jagged thing—but why should any man take a stone who had a pistol and was not afraid to use it? "If there was any sense in it, I'd say it was a fake," Reggie grumbled.

He gave up the wounds at last and moved round the body.

"Oh, you're looking at the wrong hand," Barnes said.

"Am I though?"

"Yes, this is the one where the thumb's sprained—the right hand."

"Well, you know, he seems to have been busy with his hands. What did you make of this?"

Barnes came to look. The fingers of the left hand were bent towards the thumb as if the dead man had been plucking at something.

"Not much in that, is there?"

"What was he wearing?"

"Rough brown overcoat—brown tweeds."

"Oh, ah!" Delicately Reggie extracted from the stiff fingers some little curly, black tufts.

"Well, that's queer," Barnes said. "Looks like a nigger's hair."

"You know you've got imagination." Reggie put the stuff very carefully in his pocket-book. "Some oppressed nigger from the compounds at Johannesburg—came all the way to Prior's Colney for vengeance—threw a stone at him—shot him—and then butted him. Thorough fellow, very thorough."

"What is it, then?" Barnes said sulkily.

"Seek not to proticipate. Hallo!"

The interruption was the Hon. Stanley Lomas, Chief of the Criminal Investigation Department, dapper and debonair.

"Ah, Fortune, good man. Why didn't you ask for me? I'm at the inn in the village."

"That's very haughty of you. Why not in the house? Have you put Lady Lunt's back up? Or has she put up yours?"

"Oh, best to have a free hand, don't you know? Well, what do you make of it?" Reggie shrugged. "Curious features, what? What I want to know is, was that blow on the head before the shot or after?"

"What you want is not a surgeon, it's a clairvoyant. Anyway, you don't want me. You've got your man."

"Have I?" Lomas put up his eyeglass. "You mean Cranford? Now how did you know about Cranford?"

"Sorry, Lomas. Nothing doing. I'm the independent expert this time."

Lomas frowned. "My dear fellow! Oh, my dear fellow! Unless you're acting for someone, you've no business here, don't you know."

"I'm acting for someone all right—for V. Cranford."

"Hallo! You've made up your mind?" Barnes cried.

Lomas dropped his eyeglass. "Ah! Well, well. Things must be as they may, what? It's a pity. Afraid you've made a bad break this time, Fortune. It's a straight case."

"I wonder," Reggie said.

"My dear fellow, I'd hate you to be at a disadvantage." Lomas seemed suddenly to have become older, paternal, and protective. "Well—it's not strictly official—but I may tell you we've found the pistol. It was in Cranford's rooms."

"A Smith-Southron .38? Fancy! I don't suppose there's more than half a million of them in circulation. It's a good gun. I've got one myself somewhere."

"My dear fellow!" Lomas was young and jaunty again. "Why try to bluff me? Lunt was killed by a particular kind of pistol. And we find the particular man to whom all suspicion points owns one of these pistols. It's quite simple, don't you know?"

"Yes, oh, yes, 'Doosid lucid, doosid convincing.' But I wonder why you want to convince me?"

That was the first skirmish over the Lunt case, and Reggie, Gerald Barnes discreetly excusing himself, ate a little tête-à-tête lunch with Radnor Hall—not in the silver panelled dining-room. When the servants were gone, "I don't want to hear anything under false pretences, Mr. Hall," Reggie explained. "I shall act in this case for Cranford."

"Is that so?" Radnor Hall rubbed his back hair. "I guess I'll take you right in to Lady Lunt."

Lady Lunt stood in front of the fire with a cigarette in her mouth. She was a big woman, a little flat of figure and gaunt of face, but still handsome. She thrust a hand on Reggie, gripped his hand, and shot a "Glad to see you," at him. Reggie was sorry he could not act for Lady Lunt, but had to consider that Cranford had the first claim on him. "I don't mind," she cried. It seemed her habit to be explosive. "If you're against the police, that's good enough for us. Eh, Radnor?"

"Sure," said Radnor Hall, who was watching Reggie closely.

"I want you to hear what we've got to say about the case," the lady explained. "We think it matters."

"Quite a lot," said Radnor Hall. Lady Lunt nodded at him, and he began. "You see, Mr. Fortune, Sir Albert left everything to Lady Lunt." Reggie murmured that it was very natural. "As Lady Lunt regards the proposition, it's up to her to see that justice is done about the murder."

"Justice, see?" Lady Lunt broke in vehemently. "And not have some poor devil hanged because the police think he's an underdog and don't count."

Radnor Hall frowned at her. "Mr. Fortune will realize when we make the position clear."

"Sorry, Radnor. You go on." Lady Lunt threw her cigarette away and dropped into a chair.

"Well, sir, to commence." Radnor Hall smoothed his black hair. "This firm never was Albert Lunt. It was Lunt Brothers. The late Sir Albert he was sure master. He put in the git up and git. But quite a lot of the head work came from Mr. Victor Lunt. And lately, Sir Albert having largely relapsed into living on his rents, Mr. Victor Lunt has had considerable control. Now, sir, speaking as man to man, I would wish to say that the methods of Lunt Brothers have been complex — highly complex. I conjecture that in early days Albert and Victor were both out for scalps. But in my time, Sir Albert having mellowed, largely mellowed — under prosperity and certain influences — — "

"Oh, don't blether, Radnor," Lady Lunt exploded.

"Well, Mr. Fortune, Sir Albert has lately showed a tendency to more conservative methods of finance. Mr. Victor Lunt has gone on putting in his sharp head work. There has been friction, sir — some friction. Now in this affair of Cranford's — without prejudice, I would like to say that Mr. Cranford has been hardly used by Lunt Brothers."

"He's been damnably cheated," said Lady Lunt.

"There's a point of view," said Radnor Hall. "Lady Lunt had put her point of view to Sir Albert. Well, sir, the Cranford case was largely handled by Mr. Victor Lunt. I wouldn't say Sir Albert disavowed the methods used.

But he considered Mr. Victor was taking too much control. Words passed. And we find Sir Albert shot. That's the proposition, Mr. Fortune."

Reggie smiled. Reggie put the tips of his fingers together and over them looked very blandly at the military face of Radnor Hall. "Your view is that Sir Albert was murdered by his brother Victor," he said.

Lady Lunt started and looked at Radnor Hall.

Radnor Hall gave no sign of surprise. "Pitch up another, doctor," he smiled back. "No, sir. Your guess, not mine. I'm giving out facts."

"Oh, cut it out, Radnor," said Lady Lunt.

"Well, well." Reggie surveyed her benignly. "And so Sir Albert's death leaves Victor in control of the firm?"

"Sir Albert's share comes to me," Lady Lunt said. "Five-eighths. I'm master now."

"A responsibility," Reggie murmured. "If I understand one cause of quarrel between the brothers was that Victor resented your influence, madame, which Sir Albert encouraged you to use?"

"Yes, that's the proposition," said Radnor Hall.

"You know it's not," Lady Lunt cried. "They both hated me to meddle."

"Is that so?" Reggie said dreamily. "And you were asking me to find out who murdered Sir Albert?"

"No, I wasn't," Lady Lunt flashed at him. "I was asking you to save this poor boy Cranford."

"Ah well, let's hope it's the same thing." Reggie stood up. "I can play about in the park, I suppose? Many thanks."

And he did play about in the park till dusk, and when he went back to London, Sam, the factotum, was not with him.

In the evening Donald Gordon rang him up. Donald Gordon thought Cranford was a bit of a tough, but was going to act for him. It would be a fruity case. He had arranged a consultation with Cranford at the prison to-morrow, and hoped Reggie would be there. What did Reggie think of the case? "Rotten," said Reggie, and rang off.

The fact is that from first to last the Lunt case annoyed him. He never saw his way through it, and has always called it one of his failures. The one thing which he did, he will tell you, was to grasp that the police were mucking it — to divine that whoever killed Sir Albert and however he — or she – did it, it was not a simple, common bit of pistoling. He was right about nothing else. His apology is that he has no imagination.

At this stage he was prepared to believe anything. When he went gloomily to bed it was with the conviction that if he were Chief of the Criminal Investigation Department he could make it – or fake it – into a hanging matter for "any one of the bally crowd". The unknown Cranford, the enigmatic Victor, Lady Lunt, Radnor Hall, you could put each of them in the dock – or several of them together. Lady Lunt stood to gain most by the death – or perhaps Radnor Hall – what were her relations with Radnor Hall? Cranford had the worst quarrel with the dead man – or perhaps brother Victor. In favour of Cranford was only the oddity of the business, and nice Nurse Dauntsey . . . a lamb. . . . Comfortable visions of her sent him to sleep.

Seen in the gaunt room at the prison, the unknown Cranford came up to expectation. He was a dark fellow, lean and powerful, with a decisive jaw. The little Jewish solicitor, Donald Gordon, became nervous before him. "Miss Dauntsey says I'm devilish obliged to you, doctor," said Cranford sharply. "So I am. You understand I admit nothing."

"That's the best way," the little Jew lisped.

But Cranford told his story and admitted a good deal. He had offered his discovery of copper to Lunt Brothers, and been sent out to Mozambique with a party of their men. On the way up country he had gone out of camp to shoot for the pot. Out of the bush came a native spear and broke in his thigh. By the time he struggled back to camp, there was no camp. The party had gone on with the food and the baggage, his baggage too, in which was the map of his copper belt. He was left wounded and alone in the bush. After some desperate days he struggled into a native village, and lay there a month before he could travel. When he came back to Mozambique he found that Lunt Brothers were enrolled as the owners of all the copper belt.

He sailed for England. There was in him, he confessed – no, proclaimed – the single purpose of getting his own back from Sir Albert Lunt. And so his first day in England took him to the office of Lunt Brothers. Victor Lunt received him. Victor Lunt had been civil, even sympathetic, but had nothing to offer. Victor Lunt admitted that they had jumped his claim, did not conceal that the trick had been planned by Sir

Albert Lunt, and agreed that Cranford had been damnably swindled; but gave him no hope that Sir Albert Lunt would do anything.

"You didn't kill Victor, anyway?" Reggie said.

"Victor? Poor beast, there's nothing to him. He's all talk," said Cranford. "Albert ran that show. Victor as good as told me so. Said he was just a clerk in Albert's office. So I told him a few things about Albert. Poor devil, he was in a funk. He got cold feet. Said I had better go right on to Albert. Albert was down at Prior's Colney. Would I go to Albert? I would so. And I did."

"Yes. By train. You got to Colney Road Station 12.20," Reggie said. "You came back by the 2.5."

"That's so." Cranford stared at him. "You know something, doctor. I walked up to Prior's Colney. Flunkey said Albert was out. I walked back and caught the 2.5."

There was silence for a moment. Then the little Jew said, "That's the story. You'll have to tell it in the witness-box, you know."

"Can do," said Cranford.

"That's nice," the little Jew lisped. "Now you know some fellow will ask you—don't you tell me if you don't want—did you murder Albert Lunt?"

"I did not, sir."

The little Jew rubbed his hands. "That's nice, ain't it, doctor? That gives us a free hand." He got up. "Well, doctor, any questions?"

"I wonder what coat you were wearing, Mr. Cranford?" Reggie said.

"Coat? Brown raincoat. Devilish cold it was too. Only coat I've got. I've not had time to fit out for an English spring."

"Quite. We'll carry on, then." Reggie got up too. "It's shaping all right, Mr. Cranford. Shouldn't worry."

"Not me. Tell Miss Dauntsey," Cranford said.

Outside in their car, "What's the verdict, doctor?" Gordon said.

"He's telling the truth," Reggie said.

"Fancy!" And they became technical.

On the day of the inquest Reggie went down to Prior's Colney, but the inquest he did not attend. The Hon. Stanley Lomas noticed that, and remarked on it with surprise to Donald Gordon. It was the one thing in a successful day which gave Mr. Lomas concern. But at the close of that day

Mr. Lomas, going back to the inn for his car and his tea, found Reggie eating buttered toast. "I envy you. Fortune, don't you know." Lomas sat down beside him.

"Oh, Mr. Lomas, sir," Reggie mumbled. "Go along with you."

"I envy your stomach," Lomas explained, put up his eyeglass and surveyed the buttered toast more closely. "O Lord! And after a bad day too! You've heard the verdict. What? Wilful murder against Cranford."

"And all is gas and gaiters. And hooroar for Scotland Yard. And you shall pay for my tea."

"It was the pistol did for him you know." Lomas smiled as a man who can afford to smile.

"Childhood's years are passing o'er us, Lomas," Reggie murmured. "Soon our schooldays will be done. Cares and sorrows lie before us, Lomas. Hidden dangers, snares unknown. I've found the real pistol, old thing. Good-bye."

Lomas caught him up outside. "I say, Fortune. Without prejudice — what's your line?"

"Seek not to proticipate," Reggie smiled. "This gentleman is paying for my tea, Mary. You would be so hasty, you know."

Mr. Lomas drank whisky and soda.

That was the second skirmish in the Lunt case.

The general action was fought at the assizes. The interest in it began with the cross-examination of Victor Lunt. Victor Lunt, called for the prosecution, made a good impression. He looked harassed and in ill-health, affected as a good brother should be by a brother's death. But he had command of himself, proved that he had brains as well as the heart displayed by his dull eye and flabby face, he was lucid and to the point. He showed no malice against Cranford. Cranford had called on him on the morning of the murder, complained bitterly of his treatment by Sir Albert Lunt, used violent language about Sir Albert, demanded to know where Sir Albert was, and gone away. Such was Mr. Lunt's evidence in chief.

Then arose a small and pallid barrister with a priggish nose. He would ask Mr. Lunt to carry his mind back to some earlier transactions. So the story of the expedition to Mozambique was brought out and, such was the simplicity of the priggish little man, the harassed mouth of Mr. Lunt was made to explain that Lunt Brothers had annexed Cranford's discovery, and that the expedition of Lunt Brothers had left him to die in the bush.

"Are you justifying the murder?" said counsel for the Crown.

"You will understand my friend's uneasiness, gentlemen," says the little barrister, and pinned Mr. Lunt to the statement that it was Sir Albert who had planned this iniquitous scheme. "And when Cranford had gone, Mr. Lunt, of course you warned your brother at once this desperate fellow was on his track. No? Curious. Yet you went down in your motor to your own house at Colney Towers, not much more than a mile away. You reached the house between 12 and 12.30? Perhaps? Oh, don't begin to forget things now. What did you do then?"

As far as he remembered Mr. Lunt took a stroll.

"On your oath – did you not go and meet your brother?"

Mr. Lunt (who had sat down) started up to deny it. He had not gone outside his own park.

"Would it surprise you to hear that on the path from your house to Sir Albert's there were found next day fresh footprints which your boots fit?" Mr. Lunt often walked that way. "What clothes were you wearing?" Mr. Lunt could not remember. He went as he was. "You don't deny you were wearing a coat with an Astrakhan collar?" Mr. Lunt could not say – he had such a coat – he did often wear it. "Very well. And, as you were saying, you have had quarrels with your brother about the policy of the firm?"

"Not quarrels, no," Mr. Lunt protested eagerly, and struggled to explain them away.

"On the day after the murder you had a large scratch on your forehead which was not there before the murder?" Mr. Lunt could not remember the scratch. Anybody might have a scratch. He was let go. And the jury looked at each other.

After lunch, first witness for the defence, came Lady Lunt to say that the scheme to trick Cranford had been Victor's, and that on many subjects there were bitter quarrels between Victor and Albert. Radnor Hall corroborated. Reggie followed, and brought the crisis of the battle.

Mr. Fortune, eminent in his profession, had examined the body. Clutched in the left hand were some black tufts – fragments of Astrakhan. When he visited the scene of the crime he had found on the brambles close by other tufts of Astrakhan. He had traced recent footprints which corresponded exactly to the size of a pair of Mr. Albert Lunt's boots. He produced measurements and casts. In the depths of one of the neighbouring coverts he had found a Smith-Southron .38 magazine pistol, from which three shots had been fired. And a vigorous cross-examination could do nothing with these facts. Then came other witnesses to prove that Victor Lunt had been wearing Astrakhan, and Cranford a raincoat.

Last witness for the defence—Cranford himself. Last question for the defence—"On your oath, did you murder Albert Lunt?"

"On my oath, no."

The once-confident counsel for the Crown went delicately now. It was plain enough that he thought his case did not justify him in pressing the prisoner hard. "When you were told Albert Lunt was out you made no further attempt to see him. Why?"

"I thought it was a plant. I thought the two of them were putting me off."

"So you went straight back to town?"

"Yes. I caught the 2.5. You know that." Counsel for the Crown gave it up.

A speech of sledgehammer logic from the priggish little barrister, exhibiting Cranford as a man much wronged, and Victor Lunt as the villain of the piece—a speech the more effective from its studied absence of passion. A summing up from the judge dead against Victor Lunt. A quick verdict of Not Guilty. Cheers in court. Nurse Dauntsey crying and laughing and feeling blindly for Reggie Fortune's hand.

In the corridor outside, "That's a case, my boy, that's a case." The little Jew solicitor jumped and gurgled. "Some sensation! What, Mr. Lomas, some sensation in the Yard."

"Baddish break, Lomas. 'Zeal, all zeal, Mr. Easy,'" Reggie grinned.

"Why the devil couldn't you give it me?" Lomas thrust by in a hurry. "Get on, Bell—get on." Superintendent Bell, his lieutenant, shook his head at Reggie.

That night after dinner a card was brought in to Reggie Fortune. "For God's sake see me," was scrawled above "Mr. Victor Lunt." Reggie went down to his consulting-room.

Victor Lunt was in distress. The fat face which in the morning had been pale was now crimson and sweating. He breathed heavily; he seemed swollen.

"You must expect nothing from me, Mr. Lunt. I have done with your case," Reggie said.

"You'll hear what I've got to say. You must hear my side, doctor. It was you who set them on me. My God, there may be a warrant out for me any moment. Doctor, for God's sake—you don't want to send me to the gallows. I never did it. I swear I never did."

"I have said nothing but the truth about what I found. The facts are the facts, Mr. Lunt. Defend yourself against them. I can do nothing for you."

"But the facts lie, doctor. God love you, you wouldn't go to hang an innocent man. I'll tell you the truth, by God I will."

Reggie sat down. "I can't take up your case, Mr. Lunt. I am committed. Anything you tell me is at your own risk. If you can convince me that you're innocent it's my duty to do what I can for you. But I advise you to hold your tongue."

"Don't you see?" Victor Lunt was almost screaming. "If they hang me it's you that's done it. Will you listen now?"

"Go on, sir."

Victor Lunt mopped his face, tried to speak, and stuttered. "I did go out that day." The words came in a half-articulate rush. "I wanted to see what Cranford had done to Bert. And in the park I found Bert lying shot. He had a pistol in his hand."

"Do you want me to believe he shot himself?" Reggie frowned.

"O God, I don't know. I swear it's the truth, doctor. He was lying there shot with a pistol in his hand. When I bent over him he grabbed at me. "You swine," he said, and he lifted his hand to shoot. Then I bashed his face with a stone. But he shot and it cut my head. That was the scratch, doctor. My God, you do see things. I grabbed the pistol and wrenched it away from him."

"The sprained thumb," Reggie muttered.

"Then I heard the death-rattle." Victor Lunt shuddered, and again he could not command his speech. "I lost my head, doctor. I ran away. I chucked the pistol away. I don't know what I did. Doctor, I swear it's God's truth." He started up. "What do you mean to do now?"

For Reggie sat silent looking at him. "If it's the truth, Mr. Lunt, I advise you to tell it."

"It is the truth. Don't you know it's the truth? O God!"

"I am not God, Mr. Lunt."

Victor Lunt screamed. Two men had come into the room. "Mr. Victor Lunt? I am Superintendent Bell. I hold a warrant – –" Victor Lunt fell upon the hearth.

They rushed at him, dragged him out of the fire. . . . "Apoplexy," Reggie said. "I thought it was coming." The detective's eyebrows asked him a question. Reggie shook his head.

"This warrant won't run," said Superintendent Bell. "What was he doing here, sir?"

"Asking for mercy," Reggie said. "He's taking the case to a higher court. I wonder. I wonder."

And that night Victor Lunt died. . . .

A few days afterwards Reggie gave a little dinner to Cranford and Nurse Dauntsey, and Nurse Dauntsey in a shy evening-frock was adorably happy. And in due time, "Have another peach," Reggie said.

"Do you want to see me blush, Mr. Fortune?" But she took another.

"You can do pleasant things with the stones – he loves me, he loves me not."

"It's not interesting anymore," said Nurse Dauntsey, and looked demure.

"I'm off to British Columbia next week," Cranford announced.

"Alone?" said Reggie, with his eye on Nurse Dauntsey.

"This year, next year," Nurse Dauntsey counted. "May I have five peaches, Mr. Fortune?"

"I'm sure you know what's good for you. So you're dropping the Mozambique copper claim, Cranford?"

"Lady Lunt offered to turn it over to me. I couldn't touch it."

"Of course not," said Nurse Dauntsey.

"Good thing for me Victor Lunt didn't stand his trial," Cranford said.

"Yes. It would have kept you in England." Reggie lit a cigar.

"I should have had to tell the whole story." Reggie stared at him. "Yes. That's the proposition, sir. It was the case you put up against him got me off."

"I put up nothing," Reggie cried. "Everything I had against Victor was true, and he knew it was true. That's what broke him. He had a queer story of his own though," and Reggie told them Victor Lunt's version of the crime. "I've wondered how much of that was true. He wanted me to believe Albert committed suicide, you see. And that's impossible."

"Maybe it was all true," Cranford said. "Poor beggar. He went through it."

"I didn't feel merciful," Reggie said. "Whatever was the way of it, he meant to get his brother murdered. He worked you up and sent you off to do it. He meant the murder. No, I didn't feel merciful. And yet—I wonder."

"I always meant to put you wise," Cranford said. "You'll pardon me. I couldn't afford to give anything away. And I told you no lies. I didn't murder Albert Lunt. But I killed him. Fair and clean, sir. On my soul it's as good a bit of work as ever I did. He was a yellow dog. It was up to me to wipe him out. This is the way of it, doctor. When they said he wasn't at Prior's Colney I laid to wait for him, and then I saw him coming across the park. I met him and I told him off. I had it all cut out. He had to have his chance, though he gave me none. I had two guns. One for him, one for me. I offered him the pick, and he snatched and fired at me while I had the other gun by the muzzle. He was sure trash. Then he put in another miss and I stretched him. That's my tale, sir."

"And it's just as well you didn't try it on a jury," Reggie said.

Cranford started up. "Mr. Fortune, sir, I'm considerably in your debt. But if you call me a liar ——"

"Oh, no, no."

"D'you call me a coward, then? I would have it all out if Victor had come to trial."

"You've run straight," Reggie said.

"I sure have," Cranford fumed.

"Do sit down, dear," said Nurse Dauntsey in her nice, gentle voice.

On her Reggie turned. "And you knew all the time!" He shook his head at her.

"Yes, of course, Mr. Fortune." She looked surprised.

"Cranford, my congratulations," said Reggie. "Never trust a really nice girl unless you're marrying her. Perhaps you knew that."

CASE IV:
THE EFFICIENT ASSASSIN

THERE was a silence that might be felt. The judge put on the black cap. The prisoner gave a queer cackle of laughter. And Mr. Reginald Fortune, the surgeon whose evidence had convicted him, yawned and stole out of court. The Sunday School murder, one of the most popular crimes of our generation, had bored Mr. Fortune excessively, and now that the Sunday School Superintendent was safely on his way to the hangman Mr. Fortune desired to forget all about it at once.

He stood on the steps of the Shire Hall, lighting a cigar. A large young man, who had been struggling to get in, detached himself from the guardian policeman and ran at him. "Fortune! My God!" he said emotionally. "I thought I'd never get at you. I say, come somewhere where we can talk."

Mr. Fortune looked down through his smoke with sleepy eyes. "One moment. One moment," he murmured. "Oh, ah. You're Charlecote — Beaver Charlecote. Well, and what's the best with you, Beaver?"

"It's murder, old man," Charlecote muttered.

"Everybody's doing it." Mr. Fortune frowned at him. "Who's slain now?"

"It's my father."

"My dear chap! Oh, my dear chap!" Mr. Fortune was startled into sympathy.

"I say Fortune — for God's sake — —" Charlecote gasped.

"Quite. Quite," said Mr. Fortune, linked arms with him, and marched him off.

When Reggie Fortune ambled through his four years at Oxford, Geoffrey Charlecote was one of the great men of his college, a cricket blue, socially magnificent, and even suspected of brains. The Charlecote family dated from the Victorian age. When the building of railways began, Geoffrey's grandfather was a navvy. He became a contractor, made half a million, and died. Shares of his practical ability, his originality, his driving power, and his disdain for the Ten Commandments (he was a mean old sinner) were inherited in different proportions by his three descendants. Stephenson Charlecote, his son, had one child, Geoffrey, and was also the guardian of an orphan nephew, Herbert. Stephenson Charlecote was a capable man of business. In his hands the family wealth increased. His only ambition was that the family should get on in the world. So it was Eton and Oxford for Geoffrey, Harrow and Cambridge for his cousin Herbert. Herbert emerged elegant and ordinary. In spite of Eton and Oxford, Geoffrey disturbed his father by showing signs of originality. He was bored by the big house in Mayfair, he would not bother himself with society, and he scoffed at going into Parliament. This freakish obstinacy roused the hereditary temper in Stephenson Charlecote, who was the more angry with his son because his nephew Herbert obeyed him in all things, and was successful in the most pompous drawing-rooms. The breaking-point came when Geoffrey discovered that he wanted to go abroad and be a sculptor. Stephenson Charlecote raged and decreed that he should not. And Geoffrey went.

All this Reggie Fortune, who never forgot anything when he wanted it, knew at the back of his mind. The rest Geoffrey told him as his car took them back to London.

"My God, Fortune, it's ghastly! I found him lying dead in the street outside my place. I stepped in his blood. The old guv'nor!"

"Quite. Quite," said Reggie Fortune. "Now begin at the beginning."

"What is the beginning?"

"Well, you quarrelled, didn't you?"

"He quarrelled. Oh, that sounds blackguardly. I dare say it was my fault. Yes, we had a big row. Damn it, man, what do you mean? Do you think I— — Oh, I say, this is loathsome. I believe that's what the police think. The old guv'nor!"

"Yes. But this don't help him," said Reggie Fortune placidly. "From the beginning, please."

Geoffrey Charlecote stared at him, gulped, and became more coherent. "Well, after the row I went abroad. Paris, Rome, Munich. I kept up a little place in Chelsea, too. I never saw the old man, and we didn't write. I suppose I've been a brute."

"Hard stuff in the Charlecote family. What?"

"Yes. I'm sorry, Fortune—I swear I'm sorry."

"Gut it out," said Reggie Fortune.

"Well, in Munich I married." He flushed. "You know, she's an angel, Fortune."

"Quite. German angel?"

"No. She's Italian. She came to Munich singing. And we met, and in a month we were married. I tell you, Fortune, I've been a different man since. It's as if she'd given me a soul, you know."

"Did you tell your father that?"

"It was she made me write to my father again. Lucia—she can't bear being in a quarrel. She's so gentle, any sort of bad feeling hurts her. So she brought me to try and make it up. I wrote to the old man and he answered—just a short, civil, formal note. But Lucia was sure it would lead to something, and so we came back to England. Then I wrote to him again, and he came to see us in Chelsea. That was a week ago—just a week ago to-day. He was pretty stiff and standoffish, but he took to Lucia. Everybody does, you know. Fortune, old man, she's wonderful. I thought he seemed a good deal aged, but he was just as brisk and sharp as ever. He had us to dine with him on Monday. And then—well, last night he called on us again, came about four, stayed a long time. And he was so jolly and genial. And afterwards I went out to post some letters, and there he was, lying not a dozen yards from our door. He'd been stabbed. He was in a pool of blood. Good God! It was awful."

"Yes. Yes. Seems to be a quiet street where you live."

"Vinton Place—it's a little cul-de-sac."

"It was dark when he left? And you heard nothing? Yes. I wonder who his money goes to."

"What the devil do you mean?" Geoffrey cried.

"Well, that's quite a fair question," said Reggie Fortune placidly. "If I'm actin' for you, and if you like, I will, I look only to your interests. If I'm acting for Scotland Yard—and if it's a hard case, they'll call me in—I'm only concerned to get the truth out, whoever suffers."

"And do you think I don't want the truth?" Geoffrey cried. "What are you hinting at? Do you mean I murdered him?"

"Preserve absolute calm," said Reggie Fortune.

"I'm not calm. What a beast I should be if I was calm. I want the thing cleared up, man. I want my father to have justice. Whether you act for me or act for the police it's the same thing."

"If you take it that way, I'll act for the police, Beaver," said Reggie placidly.

Geoffrey Charlecote stared at him. "That's enough, thanks," he said. "Stop the car. I won't worry you any more, Mr. Fortune."

"Mr. be blowed. Don't be an ass. Beaver. It's a bad business. Let's make the best of it."

"Will you stop the car?" Geoffrey said loudly, and stood up.

"Five miles from nowhere? Oh, go easy." But Geoffrey turned and opened the door. So the car was stopped, and Geoffrey Charlecote left forlorn in his rage on the road.

Reggie Fortune lay back and sighed. "Poor beggar. I wonder. Poor beggar," he said. And when he came back to Wimpole Street the first thing he did was to ring up the Hon. Stanley Lomas, the Chief of the Criminal Investigation Department. As a consequence you behold him sitting under the French prints in the study of Mr. Lomas.

"I thought you'd be on to this, don't you know?" Lomas said. "It's a pretty case. Wealthy old gentleman, impecunious heirs, sudden death. That's natural enough. But impecunious heirs don't stab much — not in England."

"Yes. You're intelligent, Lomas. But you're prejudiced. You always believe in the obvious."

"The obvious is what happens."

"Oh, Peter! If it did, we wouldn't want a Criminal Investigation Department. Well, now, this is what I've got. Check it, please. Geoffrey quarrelled with the old man — went away, commenced artist, and married an Italian girl — at her wish tried to make it up with the old man — old man was willing, called on Geoffrey twice, and after the second visit Geoffrey found him stabbed and dead just outside."

"That's all right," Lomas nodded. "An odd thing is, just before the murder the old man remade his will in favour of Geoffrey. When they quarrelled, he had a will drawn up which left everything to the nephew Herbert. Under this last will Herbert gets twenty thousand, and all the rest goes to Geoffrey. It was only signed on the morning of the murder."

"There's a deuce of a lot of unknown quantities in this equation," Reggie said. "Silly, futile things facts are. This set will do for anything you please. As soon as he knew the will was in his favour, Geoffrey does the old man in. Or when he heard there was a new will cutting him out, Herbert sees red and knifes the old man. By the way, Lomas, I suppose the old boy was stabbed?"

"What? Oh, damme, don't be clever. He was stabbed all right. The divisional surgeon and his own doctor, Newton, they both went over the body. Stabbed in the throat. We've got the weapon, too. Sort of stiletto or dagger."

Reggie cocked an eye at the head of the Criminal Investigation Department. "Sounds Italian," he murmured.

"It is Italian."

"And Geoffrey married an Italian wife."

"An Italian singer—a singer at cafes. That's the kind she was. Yes, that's the proposition."

"Lomas, old thing, you ought to write melodramas. The diabolical Italian singer, she leapt out of the dark, she pulled a d—dagger from her stocking, and she fell upon the dear, kind old gentleman and left him weltering in his gore. Then she put the dagger down, so the gifted detective could find it, and went back to dinner."

"It is silly, isn't it?" Lomas grinned. "But there it is, don't you know?"

"I don't know," said Reggie Fortune." I don't know anything. I was born of poor common-sensible parents, and this is all crazy. I suppose he really was stabbed?"

"You will harp on that. Go and look at him in the morning. Hang it, man, the family doctor and the divisional surgeon they ought to know if there's a hole in him or not."

"But why—why? Geoffrey—the Italian wife—they were on velvet anyway. The disappointed nephew—well, I suppose he still had his allowance while the old man lived. Do you know anything about Nephew Herbert?"

"Man about town—Society tame cat—usual vices, what? Plays a bit high. He's nothing in particular."

"Don't sound like a lurking stabber," Reggie admitted.

"People don't do these things. That's the trouble. Queer case."

"I suppose the old man hadn't a lurid past?"

Lomas shook his head. "Most respectable old bird."

Reggie stood up and gave himself a full glass of soda water. "The extraordinary efficiency of the assassin," he said carefully. "Lomas, old dear, observe the extraordinary efficiency of the assassin. Mr. S. Charlecote comes out of his son's house. A few yards from the door somebody kills him so quickly, so neatly, that he don't make one sound. And then this extraordinarily efficient assassin leaves his dagger for you to find."

"Who says he didn't make a sound?"

"Yes. Geoffrey and his angel wife. Yes. Only them and no one else. That's a flaw. Little essays in the obvious by S. Lomas. Well, it's me for the corpse, then."

And so in the morning he called at the mortuary. He was slightly surprised to find the divisional surgeon and Dr. Newton waiting for him. He returned thanks. "Is there anything to which you'd like to draw my attention, gentlemen?"

"It's a plain case, to my mind," said the divisional surgeon.

"I am always glad to have a specialist's opinion," said Dr. Newton. "Of course, this sort of thing is rather out of my line. I confess I can hardly approach it calmly."

"Quite. Quite. Most distressin'. I suppose you knew him well, doctor?"

"An old patient, Mr. Fortune. I may say an old friend."

"Ah, yes. You know the family, of course."

"They were once such an affectionate family," said Dr. Newton. "It's really terrible." He sighed. He was a florid, bearded man with a sentimental expression and manner. "Poor Charlecote! He never seemed to bear up after Geoffrey broke with him. But who would have thought that strange escapade would have ended like this?"

"So you think Geoffrey did the trick?"

"I beg your pardon!" Dr. Newton was horrified. "You put words into my mouth, Mr. Fortune. No, no. A most invidious suggestion."

"Murder's rather an invidious business," said Reggie placidly. "Come, doctor, what do you think of Geoffrey?"

"I have never been able to conceal from myself, Mr. Fortune, that there is an odd strain in Geoffrey, as it were something abnormal or thrawn—a certain violence of temperament."

"In the blood, perhaps."

"Perhaps. And yet there was nothing of it in his father. Or in his cousin Herbert."

"Cousin Herbert. Yes. What about Cousin Herbert?"

Dr. Newton laughed. "Frankly, Mr. Fortune, you baffle me. Because there is nothing about Herbert. A very worthy young man, no doubt, but colourless, quite colourless." Reggie nodded. "No." Dr. Newton pursued his own train of thought. "In my own speculations on the affair—this most deplorable affair—I find myself continually confronted by an unknown quantity, a mysterious entity, Geoffrey's Italian wife."

"Ah, there you have it," said the divisional surgeon heartily.

Reggie looked at them, nodded, and without more talk led the way to the body. It did not occupy him long. Two wounds had sufficed to make an end of Stephenson Charlecote. One in the throat, which had pierced the carotid artery; one in the chest, which had reached the heart.

Superintendent Bell, in attendance from Scotland Yard, produced the weapon found by the body—a long, thin dagger or stiletto, obviously capable of causing the wounds, obviously Italian in origin.

Reggie finished his examination and turned to the two doctors, who were waiting on him reverently. "Anything in particular occur to you, gentlemen?"

"Quite straightforward, I think." The divisional surgeon shrugged. "Technically speaking, a very neat bit of work."

"I would go even further," said Dr. Newton. "The crime seems to have been committed with remarkable skill and determination."

"The extraordinary efficiency of the assassin," Reggie murmured. "Yes. Touched the spot every time."

"It would almost seem to suggest some experience in the use of this weapon," said Dr. Newton.

"That is indicated." Reggie nodded at him. "Yes. Deceased been in good health lately?"

"I have been treating him for some time for gastric trouble—a persistent gastric catarrh. It was troublesome, but hardly serious."

And upon that Reggie got rid of them and was left alone with Superintendent Bell. Superintendent Bell cocked an oldish but still bright eye. "And the next thing, sir?" said he.

"I am feeling depressed, Bell. Do you ever have feelings? I feel this is all wrong."

"Well, sir, the evidence is thin, very thin."

"Evidence? Oh, my aunt, we haven't come to evidence yet. I'm uncomfortable. Everything seems wrong way up. Why did anybody kill the old man? He was making friends with Geoffrey again and anyway he had enough to live on. Herbert had an allowance and something of his own, too. Nobody else stood to gain by his death."

"If you leave out the Italian girl, sir."

"It keeps coming back to her," Reggie said mournfully. "But why? Suppose he was nasty to her when he called. Would she run out and stab him in the street? I wonder. Did he know some horrid secret about her past? What is her past, Bell?"

"Pretty short, sir, anyway. She's not more than eighteen. She was a café singer, all right. But we have nothing against her. In my experience they're no worse than others."

"And that's that. Have you seen his papers?"

"Better come up to the house, sir. His solicitor will be there. But I understand there's nothing in them. Very few private papers at all."

"Well, well. I suppose he was murdered."

Superintendent Bell stared. "Mr. Lomas said you were harping on that. Pretty clear, sir, isn't it?"

"I suppose so," said Reggie drearily. "But it's all wrong, Bell, it's all wrong."

At the dead man's house, his solicitor, old Sir Thomas Long, was busy in the library, and helping him, to Reggie's surprise, was Herbert Charlecote. Herbert revealed himself as a pallid, dandyish man, punctiliously polite. Colourless — Dr. Newton hit him off to the life.

Herbert was very gratified to make Mr. Fortune's acquaintance.

"I don't know whether to hope you can throw any light on this miserable affair, sir?"

Reggie shook his head. "Your uncle was stabbed, and died immediately of the wounds. That is the whole case, Mr. Charlecote. I suppose you can't help us?"

"I am bewildered. Quite dazed, Mr. Fortune."

Reggie nodded and lingered, and Herbert discreetly left him with the solicitor.

"Well, Mr. Fortune?" Sir Thomas took off his glasses and pursed his lips.

"Nothing. Well, Sir Thomas?"

"Nothing, sir."

"Ah. That was a little odd, wasn't it?" Reggie nodded at the door by which Herbert had gone out.

"Mr. Herbert Charlecote offered to help me. He used to act as his uncle's secretary. It was hardly for me to point out that there might be objections, if he was afraid of none."

"Does he know of the new will?"

"Neither he nor his cousin Geoffrey. Mr. Herbert, I infer, believes himself sole heir, and Mr. Geoffrey believes himself disinherited."

"And yet, just after the new will is made the old man is murdered! Oh, it's all wrong," Reggie said peevishly.

"An odd case. A very odd case, Mr. Fortune." Sir Thomas put on his eyeglasses again. "But I'm afraid I can't help you."

Superintendent Bell opened the door. But Reggie seemed reluctant to go, and on the stairs he loitered so much that the Superintendent turned —

"Anything doing, sir?"

"That gastric catarrh," Reggie murmured. "Let's see the valet."

The valet, an oldish man, was found. He testified that Mr. Charlecote had been much upset by the quarrel with Geoffrey. Mr. Charlecote had complained a good deal about his health. But there were no particular symptoms. Dr. Newton had been attending him for a long while. But the valet did not think that he had done Mr. Charlecote any good. For one thing, Mr. Charlecote did not take his medicine. There had been a good deal of medicine. Mr. Charlecote's instructions were always to pour it down the sink.

"And that's that," said Reggie as they went out.

"We don't get anywhere, sir, do we?" the Superintendent sympathized. "Anything you suggest?"

"How does it strike Superintendent Bell?"

"Looks like a bad case, sir. One of those where the criminal has all the luck. Verdict, persons unknown."

"So Scotland Yard leaves it at that?"

"Unless Mr. Fortune has something up his sleeve."

"Nary card. But you know we've missed something, Bell."

"Have we, indeed, sir? And where shall we look for it?"

"Oh, watch out. Watch everybody."

"Life is short, sir," said Superintendent Bell gloomily, and with that they parted.

The Superintendent was a true prophet. The sensational inquest upon Stephenson Charlecote ended in an unsatisfactory verdict of murder by some person or persons unknown. It was obvious that public opinion, and the coroner, as the voice thereof, directed suspicion against Geoffrey. He made a bad witness. He was agitated, nervous, and under the coroner's hostile examination lost his temper.

When he was asked if he knew that his father had on the morning of the murder made a will leaving everything to him, he displayed a violent agitation, swore (not merely as a witness but with profane oaths) that he knew nothing about it, insulted the coroner, and roared out a declaration that he would not touch the money, which disgusted everybody as a bit of false melodrama. If distrust and dislike were grounds for hanging a man, the jury would have made an end of Geoffrey, but the evidence, as Lomas complained, could not hang a yellow dog.

And the next day, Reggie Fortune, bland as ever, called on Geoffrey. It was a very humble house in a Chelsea cul-de-sac. The aged servant who took in Reggie's name left him on the doorstep, from which he had the glimpse of a narrow bare hall and uncarpeted stairs. He was kept waiting some time, and heard confused noises. When at last he was shown into the studio he met signs of storm. Geoffrey was flushed and visibly in the sulkiest of tempers, his wife pale and tired.

"Well, what is it now?" Geoffrey growled.

His wife smiled. "Mr. Fortune? That is so kind. If you would please sit down. Some tea, yes?"

And Reggie was saying to himself. "Oh, my aunt! She isn't a woman, she's a child." For Lucia Charlecote was so frail, of such a simplicity, that she looked rather like an angel in one of the primitive Italian pictures than a woman.

"Shut up, Lucia," Geoffrey growled. "What do you want here, Mr. Fortune? Trying a bit of your detective work?"

"You're rather difficult, aren't you?" Reggie said mildly. "You know, you told me you wanted to have the truth brought out, justice for your father, all that sort of thing. Well, I'm still on it."

"Much good you've done, haven't you?"

"I don't mind confessin' we've missed something."

"Missed! Yes, you haven't quite hanged me, thanks. You've only made everybody think I murdered my father. And so that don't satisfy you! Thanks very much!"

"Well, are you satisfied?" said Reggie. "You know, you're not fair. I'm makin' every allowance. But you're not fair. If you want the thing cleared up, you've got to give us something more. And that's why I'm here. Now, is there anything new?"

"Oh, go to the devil!"

"Geoffrey!" Lucia, standing behind him, touched his shoulder. "Mr. Fortune is very kind. He desires to help us," and she smiled and nodded at Reggie.

"Oh, hold your tongue, baby. Mr. Fortune's a damned tricky policeman, and he can take his tricks to another market."

"But you are impossible!" Lucia cried. "Mr. Fortune, you see what I have to live with. This great bear!" She rumpled Geoffrey's hair, and he made an exclamation of disgust and dashed her hand away. "But yes, Mr. Fortune, there is something new. This great animal, he desires not to take his father's money. He writes to the lawyer to say he will not have it. But I forbid him. I say it is mad. Say if I am right, Mr. Fortune. What is the father's it is the son's. And Geoffrey, he has done nothing. But if he says he will not take it" — she made a fine theatrical gesture — "people will think it is because he is guilty. Is it not, Mr. Fortune?"

"Why can't you hold your tongue?" Geoffrey snarled at her, and turned to glare at Reggie. "There's a pretty story for you. And what's your beastly detective trade make of that?"

73

"You know, Mrs. Charlecote, he's always in such a hurry," Reggie said confidentially. "Very disturbin', isn't it? You are difficult, Charlecote, old thing. Is your mind capable of receivin' a thought? Yes. Well just suppose that I may have refused to act for you, because it would be better for the son and heir I shouldn't be actin' to his order."

"What the deuce do you mean?"

"Well, I don't quite know, you know. Do you? Is there anything you really want to tell me?"

"I never want to see you again."

"Geoffrey!" his wife protested.

"Oh, he's not chatty this afternoon, Mrs. Charlecote. So sorry." Reggie extricated himself from her offers of tea, and slid away.

But he was annoyed. Against his will, the opinion of Dr. Newton forced itself into his mind. "An odd strain in Geoffrey, as it were something abnormal or thrawn, a certain violence of temperament." It was so. Confound the oily old family doctor. Why did Geoffrey want to give up the money? Mere quixotry? A passionate desire to clear himself from the ill-fame of profiting by the old man's death? Probably, oh, probably. But there was a feeling called remorse found in human nature. And why did the angel wife tell Geoffrey to keep the money? She ought to want her husband clear of ill-fame. You would expect a woman to care more about that than the man himself. And you would expect a woman to share her husband's rage with the horrid man who had not stuck up for him. Instead of which the angel wife was very anxious to keep on good terms with that horrid man. Because he represented the police? Or why else? She had a dubious way with her, the angel wife.

Reggie was worried—a rare state for him—and he took himself to his least sociable club. He was sitting there, glowering at a scientific American paper, when the voice of Lomas addressed him.

"Care killed a cat, Reginald. Why so blue?"

Reggie sat up. "Life is real, life is earnest, Lomas. And the grave is not the goal. That's because of our filthy profession, which is always bothering the corpses. Come away. I am worried. I am going to worry you."

As they walked in St. James's Park, Reggie told him of the queer talk in the studio. "I want comfort, Lomas, old thing," he concluded. "Comfort me."

74

"My dear Fortune! It's quite clear, what? Unsatisfactory case, profoundly unsatisfactory. But it's quite clear. I always thought those two were in it. Probably the sweet young wife did it, or put Geoffrey up to it. Now he funks and she doesn't. Women carry off these things better than men, don't you know?"

"I don't know. I don't know anything. Lomas, old dear, you are grateful and comfortin', you really are. I knew you'd say that. And I know it's all wrong."

"My poor dear fellow! You never will reconcile yourself to an unsatisfactory case. It's so common too—a case you can't act on while you know its sound."

"Oh, Peter! You can always act on a sound case."

"You're so young," Lomas smiled indulgently.

"We've missed something, don't you see?"

"And what have we missed, Reginald?"

Reggie pulled him up and looked at the ducks. For a long time he looked at the ducks. Then, "Cousin Herbert," he said. "The evasive, elusive Cousin Herbert. Why do we never come up against Cousin Herbert?"

"Because he had nothing to do with it, what?"

"Because we haven't looked for him."

Lomas gave an impatient laugh. "This is absurd, my dear fellow. That pallid, tame cat of a man!"

"You let some of your fellows sniff round him."

"My dear Fortune! Of course they have. He's quite a blameless sort of fellow. Plays a bit, spends a bit—nothing more."

"Oh, he wanted money—did he?"

"My dear Fortune, you're right off the wicket. He had an alibi. He was with some people at Maidenhead at the time of the murder."

"Oh, my aunt, anybody can have an alibi," Reggie grumbled.

Lomas laughed and shook his head. "It won't do, Reginald. Don't try to be subtle."

"Well, that isn't your complaint," Reggie snarled, and for once they parted in nasty tempers.

Three days afterwards a telephone message called him to Scotland Yard, and he found Lomas in conference with Superintendent Bell.

"Ah, here's the prophet," Lomas smiled. "Do you remember — in the Charlecote murder — you backed Herbert both ways? Well, the latest from the course is that Herbert has vanished."

"Then it's damned careless of you. I told you to watch him. You're not intelligent in the force, but, hang it, you might be active."

"His valet reports him disappeared. He had a dinner engagement last night. Didn't come home to dress for it. Didn't come home at all. He went out after lunch yesterday, and hasn't been seen since."

Reggie sat down. "One of your larger cigars would do me good, Lomas," he said, and helped himself. "Oh, Mr. Lomas, sir, this is so sudden. Cousin Herbert was feeling nervous, no doubt. But why this dramatic exit? What gave Cousin Herbert cold feet yesterday?"

Superintendent Bell coughed. "I was wondering, sir, if Mr. Fortune had taken any steps on his own with regard to Herbert. To alarm him, so to speak."

"Nary step. Why the blazes didn't you watch him?"

"After all, sir, we've not a thing against him."

"Not now?"

"Well, sir, it's not criminal to disappear. But I don't mind saying its odd, quite odd."

"Oh, I expect Geoffrey and the angel wife murdered him too. Just to round it off, Lomas, old thing."

"You're very merry and bright," Lomas grumbled. "I wish you'd tell me how this helps us. Why should he bolt now?"

"There is another unknown quantity somewhere," Reggie admitted.

The telephone claimed Lomas. He took it up, and his face was eloquent as he listened. He put it down again very gently. "Afraid you're right out of it, Fortune. Herbert Charlecote didn't bolt. Herbert Charlecote has been found drowned in the Basingstoke Canal."

"Good Lord, sir!" the Superintendent exclaimed.

"Pretty conclusive, what?" Lomas shrugged.

"And why the Basingstoke Canal?" said Reggie placidly. "Lots of nice places to drown in nearer home. I ask you, why the Basingstoke Canal?"

Lomas and his Superintendent looked at each other. "It really is a crazy case," Lomas said slowly, "I don't quite — —"

76

Reggie jumped up. "Oh, come on. Let's go and look at him. My car's outside. Where is he?"

"Woking. Half a minute." Lomas rang his bell and turned to his papers. So Reggie went down first. He dismissed his chauffeur with some long instructions, and himself took the chauffeur's seat. Superintendent Bell joined him. "Darker and darker, sir, isn't it?"

"Changeable weather," Reggie said. "Come on, Lomas, all aboard! Are we downhearted? No!" The car shot forward. And when it stopped in Woking:

"Is my hair white, Fortune?" Lomas said.

The two stood humbly aside while the expert was busy with the corpse. "As often as I've seen this game, sir, I'll never like it," Bell said, and Lomas nodded. But Reggie Fortune whistled as he worked.

When he turned from the body and put a scrap of something in his pocket-book—"Well, what is it?" Lomas said. "He was drowned, I suppose?"

"He was drowned all right—about tea-time last night. Say at dusk. Now for the scene of death. Where is it?"

"Just by a bridge on a by-road somewhere between here and Byfleet Station."

"I ask you, why does a gentleman of fashion about to commit suicide come and look for a bridge on a by-road somewhere between here and Byfleet Station?"

"Somebody's took some pains in this Charlecote business," the Superintendent said.

Reggie laughed. "The Superintendent touches the spot—as ever. Come on!"

He stopped his car some distance from the bridge, and they went forward on foot.

"There's a big car been over here," Bell said. "Yet you wouldn't think it was much of a motor road." It was a narrow gravel road and very loose. Just below the steep pitch of the bridge a car had been stopped, and in stopping or starting again had torn up the loose gravel. Thence to the canal was only half a dozen yards. The path was much trampled and the grass and bushes by the bank beaten down. "All that may have been done fishing him out," Bell said. "But that don't explain the car. They took him off in a wood cart. I suppose since motors were invented there never was one came down this road and stopped just here."

"Not till last night," Lomas nodded.

"So somebody," said Reggie, "somebody put Herbert in a car, brought him down here, and chucked him in. Who was somebody? Geoffrey and the angel wife, eh, Lomas, old thing?"

"Somebody put in some fine work, what? He wouldn't have been found for weeks or for ever, but a barge came along and stirred him up. And they don't have a barge along here once a month."

"Yes, there's plenty of brains about somewhere. Well, let's get busy. Herbert's happy home comes next."

The car again broke the law on the way back.

Herbert Charlecote had lived in a big block of flats several stories up.

"Did himself pretty expensively, don't you know," Lomas said, looking round the elaborate room.

"He's paid for all now, sir," said Superintendent Bell.

"Do you know, I don't feel sentimental about dear Herbert's doom," Reggie smiled. "You'd better get on to his papers. I want a man on the 'phone," and he went out and was gone some time.

When he came back he sat himself down in the window-seat and opened the big casements. There was a low stone sill which held a box of flowers. The smell of oak-leaf geranium and verbenas came into the room. "Rather oily scents, aren't they?" Reggie said. "I'm afraid he was rather oily, the late Herbert. How are you getting on?"

"He was certainly pressed for money," Lomas said. "Here's his pass-book and a letter from his bank manager complaining that he's overdrawn again. The £20,000 he came in for under his uncle's will — he wanted it badly."

"And yet as soon as he knows of that will he goes and gets drowned. Suggestive, isn't it?" Reggie smiled.

"I'm hanged if I know what it suggests." Lomas stared at him.

"Oh, my dear Lomas! Somebody expected Herbert was going to get more than £20,000 by his uncle's death; going to scoop the whole estate. Only he didn't. So he's found dead. Can you make out from that pass-book when Herbert got into difficulties?"

"About nine months ago. He's been living with nothing in the bank ever since."

"About nine months ago. Then for nine months his uncle did nothing to help him. The murdered uncle wouldn't help the impecunious nephew. Well, Lomas, old thing?"

"I suppose you're playing some hand of your own," Lomas frowned.

Superintendent Bell came forward. "Here's a sort of betting-book, sir. He put his luck at cards in it too. He was some gambler."

"Any names?" Lomas said quickly.

"All sorts of names, sir. Nothing instructive, so to speak. You might say that's curious." He pointed to a page on which, in a large, blank space, appeared the one letter, "N."

Reggie leapt from the window-seat and rang the bell. "As ever the Superintendent touches the spot," he laughed. Herbert Charlecote's man-servant, pallid and frightened, answered the bell. "Now, my man, in one minute Dr. Newton will be at the door; you will let him in; he will ask for Mr. Herbert Charlecote; you will say nothing to him, nothing at all, and Superintendent Bell will be out in the hall to see that you do say nothing; you will show Dr. Newton in here. Go on, Bell. Look after him." He bustled them out.

"So 'N' stands for Newton, does it?" Lomas said. "How do you know he'll come?"

"Because he's just driven up in his car. Because I 'phoned to say Mr. Herbert Charlecote was asking for Dr. Newton. Now you get in there." He thrust Lomas into an inner room.

Dr. Newton, more florid than ever, hurried in, and pulled up short at the sight of Reggie. "Mr. Fortune? Oh, delighted to meet you." He was out of breath. "But I thought I was to see Mr. Charlecote."

"Did you though? That was very sanguine of you."

"I don't understand you, Mr. Fortune. Are you here professionally?"

"For the Criminal Investigation Department."

"Really, though, really?" Dr. Newton was still short of breath. "And it was you wanted to see me? Anything I can do, of course."

"You can tell me what was your little bet with Herbert Charlecote."

Dr. Newton lost some of his colour. "You bewilder me, Mr. Fortune. I am not a betting man. Pray explain yourself. And I must request you to take a different tone."

"Where is Herbert Charlecote?"

"Well, where is he?" Dr. Newton echoed. "I confess I don't understand the situation. I am told over the telephone that Mr. Charlecote wishes to see me, and — — "

"That gave you a bad quarter of an hour, didn't it? There's worse coming, Newton. Yesterday afternoon" — Reggie strolled round the table and put himself between Dr. Newton and the door — "yesterday afternoon you took Herbert Charlecote for a drive in your car. When you came to the Basingstoke Canal, a nice lonely place by the Basingstoke Canal, you clapped a chloroformed wad on his mouth, and when he was senseless you dropped him into the water and left him there to finish by drowning. It was a neat thing, Newton. But he was fished out, Newton, and I've been all the morning with him, Newton."

Dr. Newton began to laugh. "Do you really wish me to take this tale seriously, Mr. Fortune? Then I must refer you to my legal advisers. I am sure that you will see that I must." He made for the door.

"Not much," Reggie said, and stood in his way.

Dr. Newton's bland expression changed. He tried to push past and, failing, sprang on Reggie. The two locked together and swayed across the room. Reggie freed himself a moment and stooped. Dr. Newton went out of the open window. As Lomas broke into the room they heard the thud of his fall on the stones.

"Good God, did he throw himself out?" Lomas cried.

"No, I pitched him out," Reggie said, smoothing his hair.

Lomas rushed out of the room. Reggie, lounging after him, went to the telephone.

In the forecourt of the flats the body of Dr. Newton lay. Lomas and Bell and the hall porter were fidgeting with it, a little crowd on the pavement gaping at them, when Reggie arrived. "You don't really want me," he said, but he bent by the body. "It's all over. His neck's broken. Fractured skull also. But that doesn't matter."

Bell stood up and blew a police whistle.

"Don't do that. Don't do it," said Reggie irritably, his first sign of troubled nerves. "I have telephoned for the ambulance and all that. Why don't you think of things beforehand?"

Superintendent Bell was startled out of his wonted composure. "God bless my soul!" he exclaimed, and stared at Reggie.

And Lomas took Reggie's arm. "Come upstairs, Fortune, please," he said gravely.

Reggie let himself be taken up to Herbert Charlecote's room, and when he was there again flung himself down on the couch. "Thirdly and lastly," said he. "And that's the end of the Charlecote case, Lomas, old dear."

"Oh, don't take that tone," Lomas cried. "We're in a very difficult position, Fortune."

"My dear Lomas! Oh, my dear Lomas! We have emerged with credit from a most difficult case. We have tracked and caught a very cunning criminal, who, when taxed with the murders of which he was guilty, became desperate, and committed suicide by flinging himself from a fourth-story window."

"You said you threw him out."

"Lomas, dear, my little jokes aren't evidence."

"You'll have to give evidence at the inquest, you know." Reggie nodded. "You'll tell this suicide story?"

"Sure," said Reggie.

Lomas wiped his forehead. "Damn it, man, I can't leave it like this," he cried.

"Oh, don't be so pedantic. The scoundrel had two murders at least on his soul. We hadn't evidence enough to hang him. He was much too dangerous to live, and he gets his neck broke quietly and without scandal. What's worrying you?"

"And what evidence have you got?"

"Ah, now reason resumes her sway. Let's begin at the beginning. Herbert Charlecote, rather less than a year ago, was at his wit's end for money. His uncle wouldn't give him any. Remember the betting-book and pass-book. But at that time he was his uncle's heir. He arranged with the family doctor, Newton, to have the old man killed. Newton would want to be paid. Probably the arrangement was a bet. Suppose Herbert bet Newton ten thousand to one his uncle wouldn't die within the year.

Remember the 'N' in the betting-book. Newton began treating the old man for gastric catarrh. Sent him gallons of medicine. Probably that was poison. But nothing happened because the old man didn't take it. Remember the valet said he had it all put down the sink. I suspect old Charlecote didn't much care for his family doctor. The time began to run out. And then came the reconciliation with Geoffrey. There was no time to lose. If the will was altered in Geoffrey's favour, no use in killing the old man. So Newton had to hustle. He was pretty neat. He chose an Italian knife, and did the killing close to the house where the Italian Mrs. Geoffrey lived. But he did it. Remember the extraordinary efficiency of the assassin. Neat piece of surgery, that murder. And then the bottom fell out of the bucket. The will had been altered. Herbert only got twenty thousand. Hardly enough to pay his debts. And so he wouldn't stump up Newton's price. Newton would cut up rough, of course. He threatened, I suppose, and Herbert threatened back. You know, I don't fancy the late Newton was a man to take kindly to being bilked. It may have been revenge. It may have been that he thought Herbert would give him away. Anyway, he took Herbert out in his car yesterday afternoon. Now we're coming to evidence which is evidence, Lomas. Newton was out in his car yesterday afternoon. I sent my chauffeur to make inquiries. And Newton drove himself. And his car fits the marks on that road — 24 Dunois Orleans, two steel-studded Blake tyres. When they got to that bridge, I suppose Newton stopped the car, pretended there was something wrong, got down, and prepared a chloroformed wad of cotton wool. He clapped that on Herbert, anaesthetized him, and dropped him in the canal. I found scraps of the wool in Herbert's mouth and nostrils. That's the case, Lomas, old thing. Come and have tea. There's rather decent muffins at the Academies'."

"Good God!" said Lomas. "Muffins!"

CASE V:
THE HOTTENTOT VENUS

IT was a night in June. The Chief of the Criminal Investigation Department was pensive. "Did you ever want to marry, Fortune?" he murmured.

"Often; but never one at a time." Reggie Fortune looked curiously at his host. The dinner had been good, the claret very good, the cigars were of the most benignant. But still — "Why this touch of sentiment, Lomas?" said he.

"Some students say women have no minds," Lomas murmured drowsily. "But that's partiality. The trouble is, women aren't human beings. Consider the parallel case of the dog. He is intelligent. But he sets different values on things from our values. Inhuman values. Think of bones, cats, and boots. It is so also with women."

"'I love a lassie' — but she ate my best pumps. Lomas, my good child, are you merely drivelling or shall we come to something soon?"

"I am much exposed to women," said the Chief of the Criminal Investigation Department pathetically, and roused himself. "But this is a family skeleton. I have a sister, Fortune. She is intelligent. She is almost as omniscient as you, my dear fellow, and much more practical. But she can be quite maddening. She is maddening me now. Unfortunately she has no husband. She had too much intelligence. She owns a princely school at Tormouth. I believe it makes her as rich as Rockefeller. She certainly does herself very well. A month ago she wrote to me that a strange thing had happened. In the night one of the mistress's rooms had been turned upside down."

"Do they rag much at girls' schools?" Reggie yawned. "It might be picturesque."

"My wonderful sister wanted me to tell her what it meant. I'm not proud, Fortune. I know my limitations. I did not see myself in a girls' school. Especially as an official. Now she has been writing to me that there are extraordinary developments. The room of another mistress has been upset."

"They do rag in girls' schools! Another advance of women. Oh, they'll have the vote soon."

"You show levity, Fortune. My sister would not like it. This is a crime. A number of photographs were taken—photographs of girls at the school. And there is no clue to the criminal."

"The great Tormouth mystery. Leader in the *Daily Scream*—'Brains for Scotland Yard.' But the independent expert found a pink hairpin in the mouth of the dachshund next door but two and brought the foul deed home to the junior curate."

"I envy your spirits, Fortune," Lomas sighed. "You have no sister—no maiden sister."

And the desultory conversation turned feebly to something else. In fact, both men were feeling the strain of that tangled and squalid crime, the Pimlico murder. They had at last contrived to hang (you remember it) the reluctant borough councillor; but only Reggie Fortune could take a holiday. As he was going, he said that he thought of motoring in Devonshire.

"You'd better call on my sister and investigate her case." Lomas smiled sourly. "If it is a case. Sometimes I think it's a dream."

"Ragging in Girls' Schools. By our Special Commission. 'Orrible Revelations."

Lomas shook his head. "I'm afraid my sister won't take to you. She's not flippant."

"Lomas, don't be improper. A flippant headmistress. I blush."

A few days later Reggie Fortune drove into Tormouth, liked it, liked its hotel, and called on the Hon. Evelyn Lomas. Miss Lomas was her brother's sister in face and shape, correctly handsome, slight, dapper, not the least like her brother in manner. She was frankly middle-aged, brisk and direct.

"So glad you could spare time, Mr. Fortune." She sat down to her writing-table. "My brother tells me I can have every confidence in your discretion."

"So good of him," Reggie murmured. He was annoyed with Lomas. He had meant only to make friends with the good lady. It appeared that he was to be an official investigator of the silly girls' school mystery. An embarrassing position. And Miss Lomas was visibly without humour.

"You will understand that discretion is essential in this case, Mr. Fortune. Anything in the nature of publicity would be unpardonable. You look very young."

"I try to be," Reggie said modestly.

Miss Lomas coughed. "These are the facts, Mr. Fortune."

With minute and tiresome detail Reggie heard it all over again and learnt nothing new. One mistress's room turned upside down in the night, nothing spoilt or taken—an interval—another mistress's room turned upside down and a number of photographs of girls taken. Only that and nothing more. Reggie was bored, and let his eyes wander from the intensity of Miss Lomas. When at last she stopped, frowning at his lack of attention, and waited in angry majesty for him to say something—

"Are you interested in archaeology?" was what he said.

"I beg your pardon," said Miss Lomas, in an awful voice.

"I was wonderin' about this," Reggie murmured, and took up from her table a little yellowish thing modelled into something like the shape of a woman. "Fascinatin', isn't she?"

"It seems to me childish or disgusting, Mr. Fortune," Miss Lomas snapped at him. "It has nothing to do with the case. But I am afraid my affairs merely amuse you, Mr. Fortune."

"Oh, please, please," Reggie protested. "You see, you're so lucid, Miss Lomas. These odd affairs are hardly ever lucid. Anything may have to do with anything. Just consider. You tell me that in your school there has been happening something unusual."

"Extraordinary, unprecedented, and disturbing," Miss Lomas cried.

"And then I find this lyin' about—a Hottentot Venus in a girls' school—that's very highly unusual."

"The thing is just a little ivory idol," said Miss Lomas and took it from him and looked at it with disgust. It was crudely and oddly shaped, like a child's modelling.

"It's not ivory, and probably it wasn't an idol," Reggie snapped. His excellent temper found Miss Lomas trying. "It's a horse's tooth, and was no doubt carved as a doll or a work of art. But how did it come into a girls' school?"

85

"I quite agree that it is most unsuitable. I should myself call it indecent. That is why I keep it on my desk." (Reggie mastered a smile.) "It was found recently in the library. No doubt one of the girls having relations in India or Africa was given the thing as an odd savage trinket. She lost it and, recognizing that it was an undesirable thing, is afraid to claim it. As a matter of school discipline I am disturbed and annoyed. I cannot conceive that it concerns you, Mr. Fortune."

"It's the only thing that interests me," said Reggie. He was tired of the lady. "You don't understand the question, madame. This isn't the kind of trinket any one can pick up. It's a jewel. This little lady" — he handled her affectionately — "she's fifteen thousand years old. She's palæolithic. There's only a few of her in the world. Some Frenchman called her type the Hottentot Venus, because she's a little like the women of that tribe. But the woman she was modelled on may have been an ancestor of yours or mine."

"I think not, Mr. Fortune." Miss Lomas was horrified.

"We have had time to improve on her, madame," Reggie bowed. "This is the point. Outside national museums, there are only half a dozen collections which own one of these ladies. Who's the quaint savant that gives them to a schoolgirl to play with? May I see the names of your girls?"

"I only accept pupils with the highest references, sir," said Miss Lomas, overawed but fuming.

So Reggie was allowed to inspect her register. He studied it in vain. No name suggested connection with any of the few archaeologists likely to own a Hottentot Venus. He gave it up.

"Well, sir?" Miss Lomas was triumphant and disdainful. "I am very much obliged to you for your courtesy. I regret exceedingly that I have troubled you with my affairs. I need not ask you to waste any more of your valuable time on the case that I foolishly submitted to you."

"But, my dear Miss Lomas, I'm just gettin' interested," said Reggie, with an engaging smile. "You know, my first thoughts were that your children had been ragging."

"Really, Mr. Fortune! Your way of putting things! Please understand that the girls in my school do not 'rag' — as you call it. I think my sex leaves that to young men, Mr. Fortune."

"Women are so revoltin' nowadays," Reggie murmured. "I wonder — you have no new woman in the flock? No bold, bad rebel?" The face of Miss Lomas answered him. "I thought so. We must have the second solution. Somebody wanted somebody's photograph."

"But why? Why should one girl want to steal photographs of the other girls? It's nonsensical."

"Oh, it's all nonsense," Reggie agreed cheerfully. "It's gibberish till we find the key. But here's one odd thing for certain, the Hottentot Venus. I expect to find a lot more before we've done."

"Do you wish to alarm me, Mr. Fortune?"

"I'm only tryin' to keep you interested. Now all these things have happened recently. Has anyone new come to the school recently? Any new servant? Any new teacher? Well, any new girl?"

"It's very unusual to have any new girls this term. But we have had one — Alice Warenne. She came with the highest introductions, Mr. Fortune. The Countess of Spilsborough asked me to take her."

"And who are Alice Warenne's people?"

"Her father is English but lives abroad. A distinguished-looking man, obviously well off. He has friends, as you see, in the best society. Her mother, I believe, has been long dead. She was brought up in France, and speaks French better than English. But this is all waste of time, Mr. Fortune. Alice Warenne is a delightful girl — a sweet nature. I can't imagine anything against her. Pray don't form idle prejudices."

"And has anybody called to see Alice Warenne since the affair of the photographs?"

Miss Lomas showed some surprise. "Dear me, Mr. Fortune — now you mention it, yes. Her father was over in England and came down to see her a few days ago. He had another man with him, I remember."

"Another? Do fond fathers often bring a faithful friend down to see how their daughters are growing?"

"Now you mention it, I suppose it is unusual." Miss Lomas looked at Reggie with apprehension. "Still, it's quite reasonable, Mr. Fortune."

"Well — if he were a brother — or a selected fiancé."

"Really, Mr. Fortune! Alice is a child. Not more than sixteen. This other man was older than her father. I wish I could remember his name."

"So do I," Reggie agreed.

"It was nothing uncommon, I think. He was rather an uncommon-looking man — big and handsome, but artistic or Bohemian in his clothes."

"And after the fond father and the faithful friend saw Alice you found this little lady" — he held up the Hottentot Venus — "in the library?"

"It was — the day after," Miss Lomas cried. "Good gracious!"

"We are getting on, aren't we?" Reggie smiled. "But I wonder where we are getting to?"

"They saw her in the library. I shall certainly ask Alice for an explanation," Miss Lomas said.

Reggie put the Hottentot Venus in his pocket and smiled at her. "I'm sure you're much too wise. Let's say nothing till we can say something sensible. I should like to see Alice. Just 'for to admire', you know."

"The girls will be in the playing-field now."

"Delightful. Suppose you walk me through. Treat me as if I was intendin' to be a parent."

"I beg your pardon?" said Miss Lomas, with emphasis.

"Oh, I mean a fond father comin' to see if it was all nice enough for my darlin' daughter. Don't let Alice think I'm interested in her."

"Very well, Mr. Fortune." Miss Lomas went off for her hat.

The playing-field was a pleasant place set about with old oaks, in the freshest of their leaves then, through which there were glimpses of the sunlit Devon Sea. Comely girls in white, clustered, arms in the air, at basketball, or ran and smote across the tennis-courts.

Reggie paused and sank down on a seat. "This is very soothin' and pretty," he murmured. "Here are our young barbarians all at play. Why will they grow up, Miss Lomas? They're so much more satisfying now."

Miss Lomas stared at him. "Naturally they grow up," she explained. "They can't be children all their lives."

"Some of us never were," Reggie sighed. "Charming, charming. Like the young things in Homer, what? The maidens and the princess of the white arms they fell to playing at ball. Charming — especially that one. Yes. Which did you say was Alice?"

"That is Miss Warenne." Miss Lomas pointed with her sunshade to two girls arm in arm. One was a tall creature, a woman already in body and stately, with a fine, bold face, and red-brown hair that glowed.

"Why, she's a goddess!" Reggie said.

"Oh, dear, no," said Miss Lomas. "That's Hilda Crowland. Alice is the little one."

"Let's go and look at the basketball," Reggie suggested, and to do that walked across the field on a line which brought them for a moment face to face with little Alice Warenne. She was a tiny creature, and had appropriately a round baby face. She was dark and plump and dimpled. But although her hair was not yet up, she need not have been younger than her magnificent companion.

Reggie Fortune's interest in basketball was soon exhausted. They went back across the field at an angle which brought them again face to face with Alice Warenne and her imposing friend, and while they passed, Reggie (rather loudly) was asking Miss Lomas questions about the school games and the school time-table. As soon as they were out of hearing of the two girls he broke this off with a sharp, "Great friends arc they, those two?"

"They are always together," Miss Lomas admitted.

"And who is the magnificent creature?"

"Hilda Crowland? Why, she's been with me for years."

"And she's the bosom friend of this girl, who's only been here a couple of months!"

"Now you mention it, that is odd, Mr. Fortune."

"Oh, Lord, everything's odd!" Reggie said irritably. "Who is Hilda Crowland?"

"Well, her mother is a widow and very well off, I believe. She lives in Cornwall. Hilda came to me through Lady de Burgh. Of course you understand, Mr. Fortune, that that implies irreproachable family connections."

"I dare say. I dare say. Well, Miss Lomas, it's a queer case. I will take it up and go into it further. Something is being planned rather elaborately in which your school, probably a girl in your school, is concerned. It may be a matter outside your responsibilities. It may be something unpleasant."

"Good gracious, Mr. Fortune, what do you suggest?" Miss Lomas was rather excited than alarmed.

"I don't suggest anything. I have no information. The trouble is, Miss Lomas, you know nothing about your girls."

"Really, Mr. Fortune! As I have told you, I insist upon — —"

"Good references. Anybody can find good references. Did your brother never tell you about the Prime Minister's butler? He came from an Archbishop."

"Is there anything you advise me to do?"

"Be ordinary. Absolutely ordinary. I shall stay in Tormouth at present. I'm at the 'Bristol.'"

So he left Miss Lomas rather ruffled, but under that deeply gratified, because her case really was a serious case, her acumen was vindicated, her brother put to shame. Her school found her more masterful than ever.

Reggie's room at the "Bristol" had a balcony which looked on the sea. There he sat before an empty plate which had held muffins, and lit one of his largest cigars. "Now where the devil have I seen that little minx before?" said he.

Upon that question he concentrated his mind, and (omitting the adventures into blind alleys) his thoughts were like this: "Typewriting . . . why does sweet Alice suggest typewriting? . . . *Mes petites manches de satinette* . . . my little satinette sleeves . . . now what in wonder is that? . . . Oh, my aunt! She was the demure little typist in that play at the Variétés last year. What was her name? Alice Ducher! . . . Oh, Peter! A soubrette from the Variétés in a blameless English girls' school! Ye stately homes of England! Give me air!"

He took from his pocket the Hottentot Venus and contemplated her severely. "I don't know which of you is worse, darling," he said. "You or Mlle Ducher. What are you at, anyway? Lord, I wouldn't have thought she had anything to do with palæolithic dolls! What's the connection, darling?" The Hottentot Venus was naturally silent.

Reggie sighed and put her away, and began to contemplate the beauties of nature. Tormouth, you know, is placed upon an agreeable bay, its sands are white, and its headlands of a dark rock which in a flood of sunshine discover gleams of crystal amid a reddish glow. So Reggie saw them as the western sky grew crimson and the flood-tide sparkled in a thousand golden jewels. A delectable scene. It was laborious to go on thinking. Tormouth is an anchorage favoured by yachts, and though it was early summer two or three white craft lay out in the bay. Reggie went into his room and came out again to the balcony with a binocular. The influence of the evening was upon him and he felt a need of futile diversion. He focused the glasses upon the yachts. There was a big schooner and two steam-boats — one a small packet with the white ensign of the R.Y.S., the other a big craft under the Italian flag. He could not make out the names.

A waiter came to take his tea away. "I want the local paper. And do you keep Shearn's Yacht List?"

Both were brought. The yachts in Tormouth Bay were reported as *Sheila*, *Lorna*, and *Giulia*. He turned them up in the list and whistled. The owner of the *Giulia* was the Prince of Ragusa.

"This is getting relevant," said he.

The Prince of Ragusa, hereditary ruler of some ten square miles and fabulously wealthy, was known to the learned as a zealous archæologist. He was one of the half-dozen men in the world whose collection might contain a Hottentot Venus. But, unless his reputation belied him, he was very unlikely to know or care anything about a soubrette from Paris. And why should he send his Hottentot Venus to a girls' school?

"Still several unknown quantities," Reggie reflected. And yet there was the Hottentot Venus in the Tormouth School and there off Tormouth lay the Prince of Ragusa. "I think we'll make Brer Lomas sit up and take notice," said Reggie, and devoted himself to the composition of Latin prose. Thus:

"De academia sororis nonnihil timeo nec quid timean certe scio. Sunt qui conjurarint et fortasse in flagitium. Si quid improvisum vel mihi vel academiae eveniret principem de Ragusa et navem eius capere oporteret."

This he wrote on telegraph forms, and with his own hand presented to the lady at the post office, who was justly horrified.

"But what language is it?" she protested.

"There you have me," Reggie confessed. "It would like to be Latin, but I left school when I was young."

The lady sniffed but, looking at it again, saw that it was addressed to Scotland Yard, and said, "Ah, I understand."

"I wish I did," Reggie murmured. For the sense of that mysterious telegram is: "I am anxious about your sister's school, and don't quite know what I am afraid of. There is a conspiracy on foot which may be criminal. If anything unforeseen happens to me or the school, catch the Prince of

Ragusa and his yacht." "Yes. Nuts to crack for Lomas," said Reggie. And he went to dinner.

It is now necessary to employ the narrative of Miss Somers, B.Sc. On the next day there was a lecture given in the Tormouth assembly rooms by Mr. Horatio Bean, the photographer of a recent expedition to the Arctic regions. To such edifying entertainments Miss Lomas was accustomed to send her girls. Miss Somers, B.Sc., was in charge of the detachment which marched to the assembly rooms on this occasion. Her narrative, purged of emotion unfit for a female bachelor of science, goes like this: She noticed nothing till the pictures began — that is, till the room was darkened. Then two girls got up in a hurry. One of them, who was Alice Warenne, whispered to her as she passed that Hilda Crowland didn't feel very well. Alice was going out with her and would look after her. They went. At the close of the lecture, one of the attendants approached Miss Somers and said he had been asked to tell her that the two young ladies had gone back to the school.

Upon this naturally follows the report of Constable Stewer of the Tormouth borough police. To this effect: Was on duty 3.30 p.m. on the quay; motor-launch from Italian yacht came in and lay by number one steps; two young ladies came in a hurry and entered launch; gentleman who had been smoking cigar in vicinity thrust paper and half-crown into my hands, saying "Constable, wire that immediate"; gentleman then took flying leap into launch, which was already shoved off, and engine started; launch steered for Italian yacht; returned to station to make report.

The paper when examined by inspector on duty was found to bear these words: "Lomas, Scotland Yard. Two girls on *Giulia*. Me too. — F." A telegram was sent. About tea-time Scotland Yard telephoned to know whether the yacht *Giulia* was still at Tormouth. A sergeant hurrying to the harbour found P. C. Stewer back at his post watching a smudge of smoke on the horizon. About that time Miss Lomas called at the police station to ask if anything had been heard or seen of two of her girls. So we leave the inspector almost exploding with a sense of the importance of his office.

"Mille pardons, mademoiselle," said Reggie, as he arrived in the launch and grabbed at his hat and, involuntarily, sat down upon Miss Crowland. With a firm and friendly hand she assisted him to recover his balance. She was in all respects made to sustain shocks. Her grey eyes smiled at him.

A man—an oldish, solemn man who was horrified—confronted Reggie. "You cannot come here, monsieur," he cried in French.

"I dare to assure you of the contrary," says Reggie in the same language.

"This is a private launch."

"Perfectly. Of the Prince of Ragusa. It is why I have arrived. I have news for the Prince of Ragusa—news which will surprise him marvellously."

The solemn man was embarrassed. "Nevertheless I protest, sir."

"I make a note of your protest," said Reggie, and bowed.

The solemn man bowed—and seemed satisfied.

Reggie sat down beside the little Alice Warenne, who had been watching all this very demurely, a contrast to Miss Crowland, who was frankly amused. "Permit a lover of art to address you, mademoiselle," said he. "I desire infinitely to thank you for the great pleasure which you have given me."

"How, sir? I do not understand." She looked more a baby than ever.

"Your little sleeves of satinette," Reggie murmured. "Your adorable little sleeves of satinette."

And then she laughed, and Reggie knew that he had made no mistake. She was the soubrette of the Variétés. The laugh of Mlle Ducher was unforgettable. "I am a great artist, sir, am I not?"

Hilda Crowland smiled at her. "Monsieur is a friend of yours, Alice?" she said in English.

"All in good time. Only an admirer at present, darling." She gave Reggie a glance which was not the least childish.

"I dare to hope," Reggie said, and again she laughed.

They were alongside the yacht. The ladies were handed to the gangway, and Reggie went up it close on their heels. There seemed to be a deputation waiting for them on deck, a middle-aged deputation which, on the coming of the girls, bared its grey and bald heads. Two men stood out from it who lifted their caps, but put them on again, one a young fellow of a sprightly air, the other grey and grave, with a certain assured stateliness. At him Alice made a saucy curtsy. He came forward and took

Hilda Crowland's hand. "My dear child," he said in English, "be very welcome," and he kissed her on both cheeks.

She flushed faintly. "I do not understand you, sir." She withdrew herself.

"I present to you your cousin, the Comte de Spoleto." The young man smiled at her and kissed her hand. The elder man turned to the others. "Gentlemen—I receive to-day my daughter, the Duchesse de Zara." One by one they came forward and were presented and kissed the wondering girl's hand. And at the end of them marched Reggie and stood before His Highness the Prince of Ragusa, who became immediately the most amazed of men. "I do not know you, sir," he said, with intense disgust. "Who is this, Audagna?" He turned to the man who had been on the launch.

"I represent her mother," said Reggie.

A wave of emotion shook the deputation. Hilda flushed and looked at Alice, who laughed. His Highness stood very stiff.

"I have not desired that her mother should be represented," he announced.

"I cannot defend the conduct of your Highness," said Reggie blandly.

"I do not admit your right to be here, sir," the Prince cried.

"That makes your conduct still more suspicious," said Reggie.

"Suspicious!" The Prince gasped and turned upon the others. "He says suspicious!" Horror overwhelmed them all. The Prince was the first to recover his self-control. "Be pleased to follow me, sir," he said, with awful courtesy. "Hilda, my dear child." He gave her his arm. "Spoleto!"

The family party and Reggie went down to His Highness's cabin. Only Hilda was asked to sit, and in perfect calm she sat. Nothing but a shade more colour in her cheeks, a brighter gleam in her eye, confessed that her stately head deigned to take any interest in her strange situation.

The Prince of Ragusa turned to Reggie. "I do not yet know your name, sir." So Reggie gave him a card. "Mr. Reginald Fortune—a lawyer, sir?"

"I am a surgeon. But let's hope we shan't need my professional qualifications."

"It is very well. You are here to represent my wife. I do not allow that my wife has any right to share my plans for my daughter. But since you have intruded, sir, I do not choose to conceal my intentions. I have

94

resumed my control of my daughter because she is now of an age to take her proper place at my side, to perform her duty to her family, and to carry out the plans which I have formed for her."

"Admirable. And shall we hear Miss Crowland's intentions in the matter?" Reggie looked at the girl.

"Be pleased to speak of my daughter as the Duchesse de Zara."

A throb passed through the yacht. Reggie looked out of the port-hole and saw the water sliding by. "So we're off," he smiled.

"The yacht sails immediately for Ragusa. I shall not be able to put you ashore, sir. For any discomfort you undergo be pleased to blame yourself and your employer. I see a rashness in your actions which I should have expected from my wife."

Reggie chuckled. "Well, well. And, of course, you don't like being rash!"

"On our arrival at Ragusa you may, if you choose, remain and be present at my daughter's marriage."

"Oh. Shall I be present, sir?" said Hilda, with a dangerous meekness.

"My dear child!" His Highness said affectionately." Mr. Fortune — you have the happiness to be present at the betrothal of my daughter, the Duchesse de Zara, to my nephew, the Comte de Spoleto."

It was Reggie who preserved an appropriate calm. He only gave one chuckle.

"How? But — but it is incredible!" Spoleto cried in French, and recoiled, gesticulating.

The Prince flushed and glared at him.

Hilda stood up. "This is ridiculous, sir," she said, and was pale.

"Ridiculous, that is the word," Spoleto cried.

"Be silent, Spoleto. My dear child, you do not understand."

"I understand enough. You say you are my father. I think I ought to know my father. I — I do not mind knowing you. But this — it is absurd and insulting. I will not hear any more about it. This gentleman — I know nothing about him." She surveyed Spoleto with disdain. "I do not wish to make his acquaintance."

"Thank you very much," Spoleto cried.

"Hilda! Be pleased to remember that you are now to do your duty as my daughter. I do not permit disobedience."

"It's no use to talk so," said Miss Crowland. "I am not a baby."

His Highness, whose grey hair was becoming dishevelled, made a violent gesture. "English! She is as English as her mother."

"Oh. If you are going to say things against my mother I will go," said Miss Crowland. "You came from my mother, sir. I should like to speak to you."

Reggie bowed and opened the door for her. As they went out he heard Spoleto say in French, "Do you see, my uncle, this does not do," and then a storm. The house of Ragusa was divided against itself in throes.

On deck, Miss Crowland seemed to have some difficulty in making up her mind what to say. "Does my mother know about this?" she broke out at last.

"That's between you and your conscience, isn't it?" Reggie smiled.

"I haven't told her anything, but she has never told me anything," Miss Crowland said fiercely. "How did she come to send you here?"

"Some rather odd things happened at school, you know."

"Did they?" said Miss Crowland, in delighted amazement. "What things?"

"I wonder if you know who little Alice Warenne really is? She is an actress from the Theatre des Variétés in Paris." Miss Crowland laughed. "She was employed to get a photograph of you, to find out all about you, to arrange for you to be kidnapped like this, and to persuade you to come aboard."

"Monsieur is a detective!" Alice slid up between them. "Oh, but a very great detective."

"I knew all that. Except that she is an actress." Miss Crowland turned to her. "Are you an actress?"

"Darling!" Alice laughed all over her baby face. "That is the prettiest compliment, is it not, M. the detective?"

"If you think she has cheated me, she has not. She told me that the Prince of Ragusa said he was my father, and that he wanted me to come on his yacht. My mother never would tell me anything about my father. I didn't think that was fair. So I came. And now, Mr. — Mr. Fortune, what will my mother do?"

"What shall we all do?" Reggie laughed. "You're in a hole and your mother's in a hole, and the Prince of Ragusa is in the deepest hole of the three."

"Excepting always M. the detective," Alice laughed. "Look, monsieur—the beautiful England—she vanishes! Adieu, the respectable country and the nice policemen!"

"Do you imagine you are here to look after me?" said Miss Crowland fiercely.

"Think of me as a mother," said Reggie, and she went away in a rage.

"Well, monsieur?" Alice laughed at him. "You are making friends everywhere. You are content?"

"If I had a razor and a clean shirt," Reggie said.

"Alas, monsieur, I have none. I do not play—how do you call them?—principal boys. Bon voyage, monsieur." She tripped away.

It was made clear to Reggie that he was not going to be popular on board. The retinue of the Prince avoided him emphatically. The royal family remained below. He was taken to a cabin, and there dinner was served him.

"And not a bad dinner either," said Reggie, as he went on deck again.

It was dark and a moonless night. The yacht was meeting a southerly breeze and the first of the ocean swell and grew lively. Reggie had the deck to himself. He was nearly at the end of his cigar before any one disturbed his humorous meditations.

"Mr. Fortune? You amuse yourself?" It was the Comte de Spoleto.

"I can smile."

"In effect, my friend, we are ridiculous. My uncle he is a dreamer—a student. He sees a thing in his mind, it is logical, it is to his desire, and he conceives it done. He has been like that always. A temperament! He is not a man of the world."

"I guessed that," Reggie murmured.

"But what to do? The situation is impossible, my friend. Conceive my feelings. This young girl—she is fresh, she is superb as a morning in the mountains—and by me she is exposed to this humiliation. And I— whatever I do, I am ludicrous. I beg of you, my friend, believe that I feel it. Imagine my position."

"Imagine mine. You might lend me a razor. But hardly a tooth-brush."

"He will not touch land before Spain. Oh, yes, he is capable of it, my friend. But this young girl — —"

"Did you bring a tooth-brush for her?"

"There is everything for her. Maids, clothes. Oh, he has thought of everything, my uncle. He calls it her trousseau. What a man!"

"Better mutiny. Seize the yacht. Can you navigate? I can't. That was always the trouble in the pirate stories."

"Mutiny? They would all die for him. Oh, you are laughing at me. *Mon Dieu!* my friend, this is very serious. I beg of you, confide in me. You must have some plan. I promise you, I desire nothing better than to restore mademoiselle to her mother. I — —"

"Spoleto!"

They turned. The Prince of Ragusa stood at the head of the companion. "My dear uncle — —"

"Spoleto! You are a traitor. You — —"

"That is not true!"

"You plot against me with this fellow. It is incredible. It is villainous. It is treachery."

"Sir, I will take that from no man."

"Yes, you will take it. You will — —" It seemed to Reggie that His Highness was about to box his nephew's ears. Reggie let himself go as the yacht pitched. They all jostled together. His Highness vanished down the companion with a crash.

"Now you've done it," said Reggie.

Spoleto exclaimed, peered at the body lying below, showed Reggie a white face, and hurried down. Reggie followed slowly.

His Highness was already surrounded by servants and his suite.

"When you have all finished, I'll tell you where he's hurt," said Reggie incisively.

"Ah, yes, you are a surgeon," Spoleto cried. "Stand aside, stand aside. The gentleman is a surgeon. Tell me, is he dead?" His Highness had begun to groan.

"Don't be futile," said Reggie, and knelt and began to straighten out the heap. The process caused His Highness anguish. "Yes. He can't walk. We must get him to bed to examine him."

It was an elaborate process and punctuated with lamentations . . . when at last His Highness lay stripped in bed and groaning faintly, "My aunt, what a patient!" Reggie grimaced to himself.

"I think I am everywhere a bruise, Mr. Fortune," the Prince groaned. "That scoundrel Spoleto!"

"That won't do, sir. I'm sure he meant nothing," said Reggie, with admirable magnanimity. "The — the yacht pitched. Now about the elbow." He began handling it skilfully.

"Ah! Yes. Yes, it is certainly the elbow that is most painful. But my knee also gives me great pain. And my head aches violently."

"The knee. Yes. The knee is badly bruised. There may be — — ah, well, I can make you more comfortable for the time, sir. But it is my duty to tell you frankly I am anxious about the arm. I must have that elbow X-rayed at once. I am afraid there's a fracture. A small operation may be necessary. Just a screw in, you know."

"A screw in my elbow!" the Prince screamed.

"I suppose you don't wish to lose your arm," Reggie said sternly.

"Lose my right arm! Good God, Mr. Fortune! You don't mean — — "

"I mean that I must have an X-ray of your elbow immediately and surgical resources at my disposal or I won't answer for the consequences. The yacht must make for harbour at once."

"Am I in danger, Mr. Fortune?"

"I hope to save your arm if you give me the chance."

"I am in your hands, Mr. Fortune," said the Prince feebly. "Oh! If you could do something to stop this neuralgic pain in my arm — — "

In fact, Reggie had a difficult time with him, which you may think was only fair. It was very late before His Highness (who took a morbid interest in his limbs) could be got to sleep; very late — or early — before Reggie went to bed, but all the while the *Giulia* was steaming back to Tormouth, and when Reggie came on deck again "pink and beautiful", as he remarked to his mirror, thanks to a razor and linen of Spoleto's, the brown Tormouth headlands loomed through the morning haze.

Already upon deck were Spoleto and Hilda, walking together, negotiating, as it appeared, a defensive alliance.

"This is very gratifyin'," said Reggie.

"How is my uncle, Mr. Fortune?" said Spoleto.

"Still asleep, thank Heaven."

"He is not in any danger?" said Hilda.

"Well, you know, he's so anxious about himself."

"I should never forgive myself if anything happened!" Spoleto cried.

"Oh, I should, you know, I should," Reggie murmured thoughtfully. They did not attend to him.

"But you are not to blame." Hilda was interested in Spoleto. "You are not to blame for anything."

"You say that!" Spoleto cried. "Thank you, my cousin," and he kissed her hand.

"Oh, but you are absurd," said Hilda, and flushed faintly and turned away.

Spoleto made a gesture of despair. "Quite, quite," Reggie said. "So we'd better have breakfast." During that meal he might have heard, if he had listened, the full history of the emotions of the Comte de Spoleto. He escaped from them to visit his patient.

The Prince was much cheered by a night of sleep, still excessively interested in his injuries, but now hopeful about them. He gave great honour to Reggie's treatment of the case. "My dear sir, I must consider it providential that you were on board. Oh, but certainly providential."

"Well, sir, the affair might have taken a different turn without me," Reggie admitted modestly.

"Indeed, yes," said His Highness. "Good God, Mr. Fortune, and how I resented your appearance yesterday!" He became thoughtful. "I think what annoyed me most was that any one should have discovered my plans." He gazed at Reggie. "Are you free to tell me, Mr. Fortune? I am much interested to know what brought you here. Did Hilda say anything to her mother? Or is there a traitor in my camp? Spoleto — that little actress?"

"Here's the traitor, sir." Reggie took out of his pocket the Hottentot Venus.

"Good heavens!" The Prince took her affectionately. "My new palæolithic Venus."

"You left her in the library at the Tormouth School. There are not many men in the world who have a Hottentot Venus to lose. So she suggested to me that the Prince of Ragusa was taking action with regard to Hilda Crowland."

"You have a great deal of acumen, Mr. Fortune," said the Prince, and the sound of the cable broke off the conversation.

There is a hospital at Tormouth. The Comte de Spoleto went on shore to bring off its X-ray man. Reggie stretched himself in a deck chair to wait events.

They were not long in arriving. A shore boat brought off the Hon. Stanley Lomas, dapper as ever, and a woman whom Reggie identified by her hair and her magnificent figure as the mother of Hilda — Mrs. Crowland — the Princess of Ragusa. Reggie went down the gangway to meet them.

Lomas sprang out of the boat. The Princess was handed out and went up the gangway. "Good God, Fortune!" Lomas shook hands. "You're a wonder! How did you bring them back?"

"Genius — just genius."

The Princess had met her daughter who was not abashed. "Hilda! Why do you do this extraordinary thing?"

And Hilda said quietly, "I wanted to know my father."

"You make us all ridiculous," the Princess cried.

"I don't feel that." Hilda put up her chin.

"May I present Mr. Fortune, ma'am?" Lomas put in.

Reggie bowed. "I am sorry to tell you, madame, that the Prince has had an accident. A fall down the companion. He is in bed. I am waiting for an X-ray to be taken of his arm. But I assure you there is no cause for alarm."

"I am not alarmed," said the Princess. "I wish to see him."

"Certainly. You will not forget that I have told him I represent you."

"It was an impertinence, Mr. Fortune," said the Princess, and swept to the companion. The door of the Prince's cabin was shut on her.

"Jam for the Prince." Reggie made a grimace at Lomas.

"Strictly speaking, what's my *locus standi?*" said the Chief of the Criminal Investigation Department.

"Don't funk, Lomas. I dare say she'll murder him. That's where you come in."

So they were depressed till the return of the anxious Spoleto with his X-ray man. Reggie descended upon the Prince and Princess. She was sitting upon his bed. She was smiling. She kissed her hand to His Highness as she went out.

All which Reggie observed with a face of stone.

"I am infinitely your debtor, Mr. Fortune," His Highness beamed. "You are not married, no?"

"It becomes every day less probable," said Reggie grimly.

"One never knows the beauty of a woman's nature till one is suffering," said His Highness.

The X-rays were put to work on the arm, and the operator and Reggie went off to the yacht's dark room. As the plate came out, "I see no injury, Mr. Fortune," the operator complained.

"Fancy that," said Reggie.

Outside the dark room the Princess was impatiently waiting. "Well, Mr. Fortune?"

"Well, madame, there will be no need of an operation."

The Princess frowned at him. "I suppose I am much obliged to you, Mr. Fortune. I wish to hear more of your part in the affair."

Reggie, he has confessed, trembled. The Princess swept on. She opened the door of the music-room. She revealed Hilda and Spoleto. Hilda was being vehemently kissed.

Reggie fled. Professional instinct, he explains, took him back to his patient. "I am very pleased to tell you, sir, that there is no serious injury to the arm. Rest and good nursing are all that is now needed."

His Highness laughed like a boy and began to chatter—all about himself.

Reggie broke in at the first chance. "It is a satisfaction to me that I leave you in such good spirits, sir."

His Highness overflowed with gratitude. He did not know how to thank Mr. Fortune—what to offer him.

"If I might have this little lady, sir." Reggie took up the Hottentot Venus. "It would be a pleasant memento of an interesting adventure." And so he went off with the Hottentot Venus in his pocket. He hurried on deck to the uneasy Lomas. "You were right, Lomas. You are always right. We have no *locus standi*. And where's that shore boat?" They embarked hurriedly and rowed away from the royal house of Ragusa. "In heaven," said Reggie, "there is neither marrying nor giving in marriage. That's why

I'm going there. Look at her" — he produced the Hottentot Venus — "she's the only sensible woman I ever knew. Lomas, my dear old man, do you know you will have to explain all this to your sister?"

The Chief of the Criminal Investigation Department groaned aloud.

CASE VI:
THE BUSINESS MINISTER
PHASE I.—THE SCANDAL

"'OH, to be in England now that April's here,'" said Reggie Fortune as, trying to hide himself in his coat, he slipped and slid down the gangway to his native land. The Boulogne boat behind him, lost in driving snow, could be inferred from escaping steam and the glimmer of a rosette of lights. "The Flying Dutchman's new packet," Reggie muttered, and hummed the helmsman's song from the opera, till a squall coming round the corner stung what of his face he could not bury like small shot.

He continued to suffer. The heat in the Pullman was tinned. He did not like the toast. The train ran slow, and whenever he wiped the steamy window he saw white-blanketed country and fresh swirls of snow. So he came into Victoria some seven hours late, and it had no taxi. He said what he could. You imagine him, balanced by the two suit-cases which he could not bear to part with, wading through deep snow from the Tube station at Oxford Circus to Wimpole Street, and subsiding limp but still fluent into the arms of Sam his factotum. And the snow went on falling.

It was about this time, in his judgment 11 p.m. on 15th April, that a man fell from the top story of Montmorency House, the hugest and newest of the new blocks of flats thereabouts. He fell down the well which lights the inner rooms and, I suppose, made something of a thud as his body passed through the cushion of snow and hit the concrete below. But in the howl of the wind and the rattle of windows it would have been extraordinary if anyone had heard him or taken him for something more than a slate or a chimney pot. He was not in a condition to explain himself. And the snow went on falling.

Mr. Fortune, though free from his coat and his hat and his scarf and his gloves, though scorching both hands and one foot at the hall fire, was still telling Sam his troubles when the Hon. Stanley Lomas came downstairs. Mr. Fortune said, "Help!"

"Had a good time?" said Lomas cheerily. "Did you get to Seville?"

"Oh, Peter, don't say things like that. I can't bear it. Have the feelings of a man. Be a brother, Lomas. I've been in nice, kind countries with a well-bred climate, and I come back to this epileptic blizzard, and here's Lomas pale and perky waiting for me on the mat. And then you're civil! Oh, Sophonisba! Sophonisba, oh!"

"I did rather want to see you," Lomas explained.

"I hate seeing you. I hate seeing anything raw and alive. If you talk to me I shall cry. My dear man, have you had dinner?"

"Hours ago."

"That wasn't quite nice of you, you know. When you come to see me, you shouldn't dine first. It makes me suspect your taste. Well, well! Come and see me eat. That is a sight which has moved strong men to tears, the pure ecstasy of joy, Lomas. The sublime and the beautiful, by R. Fortune. And Sam says Elise has a *timbale de foie gras* and her very own *entrecôte*. Dine again, Whittington. And we will look upon the wine when it is red. My Chambertin is strongly indicated. And then I will fall asleep for a thousand years, same like the Sleeping Beauty."

"I wish I could."

"Lomas, old dear!" Reggie turned and looked him over. "Yes, you have been going it. You ought to get away."

"I dare say I shall. That is one of the things I'm going to ask you — what you think about resignation."

"Oh, Peter! As bad as that?" Reggie whistled. "Sorry I was futile. But I couldn't know. There's been nothing in the papers."

"Only innuendoes. Damme, you can't get away from it in the clubs."

They had it out over dinner.

Some months before a new Government had been formed, which was advertised to bring heaven down to earth without delay. And the first outward sign of its inward and spiritual grace was the Great Coal Ramp. Some folks in the City began to buy the shares of certain coal companies. Some folks in the City began to spread rumours that the Government was going to nationalize mines district by district — those districts first in which the shares had been bought. The shares then went to a vast price.

"All the usual nauseating features of a Stock Exchange boom," said Reggie.

"No. This is founded on fact," said Lomas. "That's the distinguishing feature. It was worked on the truth, the whole truth, and nothing but the truth. Whoever started the game had exact and precise information. They only touched those companies which the Government meant to take over; they knew everything and they knew it right. Somebody of the inner circle gave the plan away."

"'Politics is a cursed profession,'" said Reggie.

Lomas looked gloomily at his Burgundy. "Politicians are almost the lowest of God's creatures," he agreed. "I know that. I'm a Civil servant. But I don't see how any of them can have had a finger in this pie. The scheme hadn't come before the Cabinet. Everybody knew, of course, that something was going to be done. But the whole point is the particular companies concerned in this primary provisional scheme. And nobody knew which they were but the President of the Board of Trade and his private secretary."

"The President — that's Horace Kimball."

"Yes. No politics about him. He's the rubber king, you know. He was brought in on the business men for a business Cabinet cry. He was really put there to get these nationalization schemes through."

"And he begins by arousing city scandal. Business men and business methods. Well, well! Give me the politicians after all. I was born respectable. I would rather be swindled in the quiet, old-fashioned way. I like a sense of style."

"Quite — quite," said Lomas heartily. "But I must say I have nothing against Kimball. He is the usual thing. Thinks he is like Napoleon — pathetically anxious you should suppose he has been educated. But he really is quite an able fellow, and he means to be civil. Only he's mad to catch the fellow who gave his scheme away. I don't blame him. But it's damned awkward."

"If only Kimball and his private secretary knew, either Kimball or the private secretary gave it away."

"My dear Fortune, if you say things like that, I shall break down. That is the hopeless sort of jingle I say in my sleep. I believe Kimball's honest. That's his reputation. As keen as they make 'em, but absolutely straight. And why should he play double? He is ridiculously rich. If he wanted money it was idiotic to go into the Government. He would do much better for himself in business. No; he must have gone into politics for power and position and so on. And then at the start his career is mucked by a financial scandal. You can't suppose he had a hand in it. It's too mad."

"Remains the private secretary. Don't Mr. Kimball like his private secretary?"

"Oh, yes. Kimball thinks very well of him. I pointed out to Kimball that on the facts we were bound to suspect Sandford, and he was quite huffy about it—said he had the highest opinion of Sandford, asked what evidence I had, and so on."

"Very good and proper, and even intelligent. My respects to H. Kimball. What evidence have you, Lomas, old thing?"

"You just put the case yourself," said Lomas, with some irritation. "Only Kimball and Sandford were in the secret. It's impossible in the nature of things Kimball should have sold it. Remains Sandford."

"Oh, Peter! That's not evidence, that's an argument."

"I know, confound you. But there is evidence of a sort. One of Sandford's friends is a young fellow called Walkden, and he's in one of the firms which have been running the Stock Exchange boom."

"It's queer," said Reggie, and lit a pipe. "But it wouldn't hang a yellow dog."

"Do you think I don't know that?" Lomas cried. "We have nothing to act on, and they're all cursing me because we haven't!"

"Meaning Kimball?"

"Kimball—Kimball's calling twice a day to know how the case is going on, please. But the whole Government's on it now. Minutes from the Home Secretary—bitter mems. from the Prime Minister. They want a scapegoat, of course. Governments do."

"Find us someone to hang or we'll hang you?"

"I told you I was thinking of resigning."

"Because they want to bully you into making a case against the private secretary—and you have a conscience?"

"Lord, no. I'd convict him to-day if I could. I don't like the fellow. He's a young prig. But I can't convict him. No; I don't think they want to hang anybody in particular. But they must have somebody to hang, and I can't find him."

"It isn't much in my way," Reggie murmured. "The Civil Service frightens me. I have a brother-in-law in the Treasury. Sometimes he lets me dine with him. Meditations among the Tombs for Reginald. No. It isn't much in my way. I want passion and gore. But you intrigue me, Lomas, you do indeed. I would know more of H. Kimball and Secretary Sandford. They worry me."

"My God, they worry me," said Lomas heartily.

"They are too good to be true. I wonder if there's any other nigger in the wood pile."

"Well, I can't find him."

"Hope on, hope ever. Don't you remember it was the dowager popped the Bohun sapphires? And don't you resign. If the Prime Minister sends you another nasty mem., say you have your eye on his golf pro. A man who putts like that must have something on his conscience. And don't you resign for all the politicians outside hell. It may be they want to get rid of you. I'll come and see you to-morrow."

"I wish you would," said Lomas. "You have a mighty good eye for a face."

"My dear old thing! I never believe in faces, that's all. The only one I ever liked was that girl who broke her sister-in-law's nose. But I'll come round."

Comforted by wine and sympathy, Lomas was sent away to trudge home through a foot of snow. And the snow went on falling.

Phase II.—The Private Secretary

The snow lingered. Though hoses washed it out of the highways, in every side street great mounds lay unmelted, and the park was dingily white. Reggie shivered as he got out of his car in Scotland Yard, and he scurried upstairs and put himself as close as he could to Lomas's fire — ousting Superintendent Bell.

"I'm waiting for you," said Lomas quietly. "There's a new fact. Three thousand pounds has been paid into Sandford's account. It was handed in over the counter in notes of small amounts yesterday morning. Cashier fancies it was paid in by a stoutish man in glasses — couldn't undertake to identify."

"It's a wicked world, Lomas. That wouldn't matter so much if it was sensible. Someday I will take to crime, just to show you how to do it. Who is Sandford, what is he, that such queer things happen round him?"

"I don't know so much about queer, sir," said Superintendent Bell. "I suppose this three thousand is his share of the swag."

"That's what we're meant to suppose," Reggie agreed. "That's what I resent."

"You mean, why the devil should he have it put in the bank? He must know his account would be watched. That's the point I took," said Lomas wearily.

"Well, sir, as I was saying, it's the usual sort of thing," Superintendent Bell protested. "When a city gang has bought a fellow in a good position and got all they can get out of him, it often happens they don't care anymore about him. They'd rather break him than not. It happened in the Bewick affair, the Grantley deal — —" He reeled off a string of cases. "What I mean to say, sir, there isn't honour among thieves. When they see one of themselves in a decent position, they'll do him in if they can. Envy, that's what it is. I suppose we're all envious. But in my experience, when a fellow isn't straight he gets a double go of envy in him. I mean to say, for sheer spiteful envy the crooks beat the band."

Reggie nodded. "Do you know, Bell, I don't ever remember your being wrong, when you had given an opinion. By the way, what is your opinion?"

Superintendent Bell smiled slowly. "We do have to be so careful, sir. Would you believe it, I don't so much as know who did the open-air work in the Coal Ramp. There was half a dozen firms in the boom, quite respectable firms. But who had the tip first, and who was doing the big business, I know no more than the babe in arms."

"Yes, there's some brains about," Lomas agreed.

But Reggie, who was watching the Superintendent, said, "What's up your sleeve, Bell?"

The Superintendent laughed. "You do have a way of putting things, Mr. Fortune." He lit a cigarette and looked at his chief. "I don't know what you thought of Mr. Sandford, Mr. Lomas?"

"More do I, Bell," said Lomas. "I only know he's not a man and a brother."

"What I should describe as a lonely cove, sir," Bell suggested. "Chiefly interested in himself, you might say."

"He's a climber," said Lomas.

"Well, well! Who is Sandford—what is he, that all the world don't love him?" Reggie asked. "Who was his papa? What was his school?"

"Well, now, it's rather odd you should ask that, sir," said Superintendent Bell.

"He didn't have a school. He didn't have a father," said Lomas. "First he knows he was living with his widowed mother, an only child, in a little village in North Wales—Llan something. He went to the local grammar-school. He was a kind of prize boy. He got a scholarship at Pembroke, Oxford. Then Mrs. Sandford died, leaving him about a pound a week. He got firsts at Oxford, and came into the Home Civil pretty high. He's done well in his Department, and they can't stand him."

"Good brain, no geniality, if you take my meaning," said the Superintendent.

"I hate him already," Reggie murmured.

"That's quite easy," said Lomas. "Well, he's a clever second-rater, that's what it comes to."

"Poor devil," Reggie murmured.

110

"There's swarms of them in the service. The only odd thing about Sandford is that he don't seem to have any origins. Like that fellow in the Bible who had no ancestors — Melchizedek, was it? Well, Mrs. Sandford had no beginning either. She wasn't native to Llanfairfechan — that's the place. She came there when Sandford was a small kid. Nobody there knows where from. He says he don't know where from. Nobody knows who his father was. He says he don't know. He says she left no papers of any sort. She had an annuity, and the fifty pounds a year she left him was in Consols. He never knew of any relations. Nobody in Llan-what's-its-name can remember anybody ever coming to see her. And she died ten years ago."

"You might say it looked as if she wanted to hide," said Superintendent Bell. "But, Lord, you can't tell. Might be just a sorrowful widow. It takes 'em that way sometimes."

"Has anybody ever shown any interest in Melchizedek?" said Reggie.

"O Lord, no! Nobody ever heard of him out of his Department. And there they all hate him. But he's the sort of fellow you can't keep down."

"Poor devil," Reggie murmured again.

"You won't be so damned sympathetic when you've met him," Lomas said. A slip of paper was presented to him. "Hallo! Here's Kimball. I thought he was leaving me alone too long. Well, we've got something for him to-day."

"He has a large fat head": thus some perky journalist began a sketch of the Rt. Hon. Horace Kimball. And he faithfully reported the first elementary effect of seeing Mr. Kimball, who looked a heavy fellow, with the bulk of his head and neck supported on a sturdy frame. But on further acquaintance people discovered a vivacity of movement and a keenness of expression which made them uncomfortable. Yet he had, as I intend you to observe, a bluff, genial manner, and his cruellest critics were always those who had not met him. For the rest, he aimed at a beautiful neatness in his clothes, and succeeded.

He rushed in. "Well, Lomas, if we don't make an end of this business, it'll make an end of us," he announced, and flung himself at a chair. "Anything new?"

"I have just been discussing it with Mr. Fortune."

"That's right. Want the best brains we can get." He nodded his heavy head at Reggie. "What do you make of it?"

"I don't wonder you find it harassing," Reggie said.

"Harassing! That's putting it mildly. I've lost more sleep over it than I want to think about." He became aware that Reggie was studying him. "Doctor, aren't you?" he laughed ruefully. "I'm not a case, you know."

"I apologize for the professional instinct," Reggie said. "But it does make me say you ought to see your doctor, sir."

"My doctor can't tell me anything I don't know. It's this scandal that's the matter with me. You wouldn't say I was sentimental, would you? You wouldn't take me for an innocent? Well, do you know, I've been in business thirty years, and I've never had one of my own people break faith with me. That's what irritates me. Somebody in my own office, somebody close to me, selling me. By God, it's maddening!"

"Whom do you suspect?" said Reggie.

Kimball flung himself about, and the chair creaked. "Damn it, man, we've had all that out over and over again. I can't suspect any one. I won't suspect any one. But the thing's been done."

"As I understand, the only people who knew the scheme were yourself and Sandford, your secretary?"

"I'd as soon suspect myself as Sandford."

"Yesterday three thousand pounds in notes was paid by somebody, who didn't give his name, into Sandford's account," said Lomas.

"Great God!" said Kimball, and rolled back in his chair, breathing heavily. "That's what I wouldn't let myself believe."

"Have you got any brandy, Lomas?" said Reggie, watching his pallor professionally. Lomas started up. Reggie reached out and began to feel Kimball's pulse.

"Don't do that," said Kimball sharply, and dragged his hand away. "Good Lord, man, I'm not ill! No, thanks, Lomas, nothing, nothing. I never touch spirits. I'll be all right in a moment. But it does rather knock me over to find I've got to believe it was Sandford." He struggled out of his chair, walked to the window, and flung it up and dabbed at his forehead. He stood there a moment in the raw air, took a pinch of snuff, and turned on them vigorously. "There's no doubt about this evidence, eh? We can't get away from it?"

112

"I'm afraid we must ask Sandford for an explanation," said Lomas.

"Most unpleasant thing I ever did in my life," Kimball said. "Well, there's no help for it, I suppose. Still, he may have a perfectly good explanation. Damn it, I won't make up my mind till I must. I've always found him quite straight—and very efficient too. Cleverest fellow I ever had about me. Send for him then; say I'll be glad to see him here. Come now, Lomas, what do you think yourself? He may be able to account for it quite naturally, eh?"

"He may. But I can't see how," Lomas said gloomily. "Can you?"

"I suppose you think I'm a fool, but I like to believe in my fellows," said Kimball, and they passed an awkward five minutes till Sandford came.

He looked a good young man. He was rather small, he was very lean, he wore eyeglasses. Everything about him was correct and restrained. But there was an oddity of structure about his face: it seemed to come to a point at the end of his nose, and yet his lower jaw looked heavy.

He made graded salutations to Kimball his chief and to Lomas. He looked at Reggie and Superintendent Bell as though he expected them to retreat from his presence. And he turned upon Kimball a glance that bade him lose no time.

Kimball seemed to find some difficulty in beginning. He cleared his throat, blew his nose, and took another pinch of snuff. "I don't know if you guess why I sent for you," he broke out.

"I infer that it is on this matter of the gamble in coal shares," said Sandford precisely.

"Yes. Do you know of any new fact?"

"Nothing has come before me."

"Well, there's something I want you to explain. I dare say you have a satisfactory explanation. But I'm bound to ask for it."

"I have nothing to explain that I know of."

"It's been brought to my knowledge that yesterday three thousand pounds in notes was paid into your account. Where did it come from?"

Sandford took off his eyeglasses and cleaned them, and put them on again. "I have no information," he said in the most correct official manner.

"Good God, man, you must see what it means!" Kimball cried.

"I beg your pardon, sir. I have no notion of what it means. I find it difficult to believe that you have been correctly informed."

"You don't suppose I should take up a charge like this unless I was compelled to."

"There's no doubt of the fact, Mr. Sandford," said Lomas gloomily.

"Indeed! Then I have only to say that no one has any authority to make payments into my account. As you have gone into the affair so carefully, I suppose you have found out who did."

"He didn't give his name, you see. Can you tell us who he was?" Lomas said.

"I repeat, sir, I know nothing about the transaction."

"And that's all you say?"

"I need hardly add that I shall not accept the money."

"You know the matter can't end there!" Kimball cried. "Come, man, you're not doing yourself justice. Nothing could be worse for you than this tone, can't you see that?"

"I beg your pardon, sir. I do not see what you wish me to say. You spoke of making a charge. Will you be so good as to state it?"

"If you must have it! This boom was begun on information which only you had besides myself. And immediately after the boom this large sum is paid secretly into your account. You must see what everybody will say—what I should say myself if I didn't know you—that you sold the plan, and this money is your price. Come, you must have some explanation for us—some defence, at least."

"I say again, sir, I know nothing of the matter. I should hope that what that scandal may say will have no influence upon anyone who knows my character and my career."

"Good God, man, we're dealing with facts! Where did that three thousand pounds come from?"

"I have no information. I have no idea."

For the first time Reggie spoke. "I wonder if you have a theory."

"I don't consider it is my duty to imagine theories."

"Do you know anyone who wants to ruin you? Or why anyone should?"

"I beg your pardon. I must decline to be led into wild speculations of that kind."

114

Kimball started up. "You make it impossible to do anything for you. I have given you every chance, remember that—every chance. It's beyond me now. I can only advise you to consider your position. I don't know whether your resignation will save you from worse consequences. I'll do what I can. But you make it very hard. Good morning. You had better not go back to the office."

"I deny every imputation," said Sandford. "Good morning, sir."

Half apologetically Kimball turned to the others. "There's nothing for it, I suppose. We'll have to go through with it now. You'll let me have an official report. The fellow's hopeless. Poor devil!"

"I can't say he touches my heart," said Lomas.

Kimball laughed without mirth. "He can't help himself," he said, and went out.

"I shouldn't have thought Kimball was so human," said Lomas.

"Well, sir, he always has stuck to his men, I must say," said Superintendent Bell.

"I wonder he could stick to Sandford for a day."

"That Mr. Sandford, he is what you might call a superior person," Bell chuckled. "Funny how they brazen it out, that kind."

"Yes, I don't doubt he thinks he was most impressive. Well, Fortune, there's not much here for you, I'm afraid."

Reggie had gone to the window and was fidgeting there. "I say, the wind's changed," said he. "That's something, anyway."

Phase III.—The Man under the Snow

The porter of Montmorency House, awaking next morning, discovered that even in the well of his flats, where the air is ever the most stagnant in London, the snow was melting fast. After breakfast he saw some clothes emerging from the slush. This annoyed him, for he cherished that little court. The tenants, he remarked to his wife, were always doing something messy, but dropping their trousers down the well was the limit. He splashed out into the slush and found a corpse.

After lunch Reggie Fortune, drowsing over the last published play of Herr Wedekind, was roused by the telephone, which, speaking with the voice of Superintendent Bell, urged him to come at once to the mortuary.

"Who's dead?" he asked. "Sandford hanged himself in red tape? Kimball had a stroke?"

"It's what you might call anonymous," said the voice of the Superintendent. "Just the sort of case you like."

"I never like a case," said Reggie, with indignation, and rang off.

At the door of the mortuary Superintendent Bell appeared as his car stopped.

"You're damned mysterious," Reggie complained.

"Not me, sir. If you can tell me who the fellow is, I'll be obliged. But what I want to know first is, what was the cause of death. You'll excuse me, I won't tell you how he was found till you've formed your opinion."

"What the devil do you mean by that?"

"I don't want you to be prejudiced in any way, sir, if you take my meaning."

"Damn your impudence. When did you ever see me prejudiced?"

"Dear me, Mr. Fortune, I never heard you swear so much," said Bell sadly. "Don't be hasty, sir. I have my reasons. I have, really."

He led the way into the room where the dead man lay. He pulled back the sheet which covered the body. "Well, well!" said Reggie Fortune. For the dead man's face was not there.

116

"You'll excuse me. I shouldn't be any good to you," said the Superintendent thickly, and made for the door.

Reggie did not look round. "Send Sam in with my things," he said.

It was a long time afterwards when, rather pale for him, his round and comfortable face veiled in an uncommon gravity, he came out.

Superintendent Bell threw away his cigarette. "Ghastly, isn't it?" he said with sympathy.

"Mad," said Reggie. "Come on." A shower of warm rain was being driven before the west wind, but he opened everything in his car that would open, and told the chauffeur to drive round Regent's Park. "Come on. Bell. The rain won't hurt you."

"I don't wonder you want a blow. Poor chap! As ugly a mess as ever I saw."

"I suppose I'm afraid," said Reggie slowly. "It's unusual and annoying. I suppose the only thing that does make you afraid is what's mad. Not the altogether crazy—that's only a nuisance-but what's damned clever and yet mad. An able fellow with a mania on one point. I suppose that's what the devil is, Bell."

"Good Lord, sir," said Superintendent Bell.

"What I want is muffins," said Reggie—"several muffins and a little tea and my domestic hearth. Then I'll feel safe."

He spread himself out, sitting on the small of his back before his study fire, and in that position contrived to eat and drink with freedom.

"In another world, Bell," he said dreamily—"in another and a gayer world it seems to me you wanted to know the cause of death. And you didn't want me to be prejudiced. Kindly fellow. But there's no prejudice about. It's quite a plain case."

"Is it indeed, sir? You surprise me."

"The dead man was killed by a blow on the left temple from some heavy, blunt weapon—a life-preserver, perhaps; a stick, a poker. At the same time, or immediately after death, his face was battered in by the same or a similar weapon. Death probably occurred some days ago. After death, but not long after death, the body received other injuries, a broken rib and left shoulder-blade, probably by a fall from some height. That's the medical evidence. There are other curious circumstances."

117

"Just a few!" said Bell, with a grim chuckle. "You're very definite, sir, if I might say so. I suppose he couldn't have been killed and had his face smashed like—like he did—by the fall?"

"You can cut that right out. He was killed by a blow and blows smashed his face in. Where did you find him?"

"He was found when the snow melted this morning in the well at Montmorency House."

"Under the snow? That puts the murder on the night of the fifteenth. Yes, that fits; that accounts for his sodden clothes."

"There's a good deal it don't account for," said Bell gloomily.

"I saw him just as he was found?" Bell nodded. "Somebody took a lot of pains with him. He was fully dressed—collar and tie, boots. But a lot of his internal buttons were undone. And there's not a name, not even a maker's name, on any of his clothes. His linen's new and don't show a laundry mark. Yes, somebody took a lot of pains we shouldn't know him."

"I don't know what you're getting at, sir."

"Don't you? Is it likely a man wearing decent clothes would not have his linen marked and his tailor's name somewhere? Is it likely a man who had his tie and collar on wouldn't do up his undershirt? No. The beggar's clothes were changed after he was killed. That must have been a grisly business too. He's not a tender-hearted fellow who did this job. Valet the body you've killed and then bash its face in! Well, well! Have some more tea?"

"Not me," said Bell, with a gulp. "You talked about a madman, sir, didn't you?"

"Oh, no, no, no. Not the kind of mad that runs amuck. Not homicidal mania. This isn't just smashing up a chap's body for the sake of smashing. There's lots of purpose here. This is damned cold, calculating crime. That kind of mad. Some fellow's got an object that makes it worthwhile to him to do any beastliness. That's the worst kind of mad, Bell. Not homicidal mania—that only makes a man a beast. What's here is the sort of thing that makes a man a devil."

"You're going a bit beyond me, sir. It's a bloody murder, and that's all I want."

"Yes, that's our job," said Reggie thoughtfully. Together they went off to Montmorency House.

118

"How would you describe deceased, sir?" said Bell.

"Man of about fifty, under middle height, inclined to be stout, unusual bald."

"It ain't much to go by, is it?" Bell sighed. "We don't so much as know if he was clean shaved or not."

"He was, I think. I saw no trace of facial hair. But it's rash to argue from not finding things. And he might have been shaved after he was killed."

"And then smashed? My Lord! And they smashed him thorough too, didn't they?"

"Very logical bit of crime, Bell."

"Logical! God bless my soul! But I mean to say, sir, we haven't got much to go on. Suppose I advertise there's a man of fifty missing, rather short and stout and bald, I shall look a bit of an ass."

"Well, I wouldn't advertise. He'd had an operation, by the way—on the ear. But I wouldn't say that either. In fact, I wouldn't say anything about him just yet. Hold your trumps."

"Trumps? What is trumps then, Mr. Fortune?"

"Anything you know is always trumps."

"You'll excuse me, but it's not my experience, sir."

They came to Montmorency House, where detectives were already domesticated with the porter, and had done the obvious things. The body, it was to be presumed, had fallen from one of the windows opening on the well. The men who had flats round the well were all accounted for, save one. Mr. Rand, tenant of a flat on the top story, had not been seen for some days. Ringing at Mr. Rand's door had produced no reply.

"Well, we do seem to be getting a bit warmer," said Superintendent Bell. And his subordinate in charge of the inquiries at the flats beamed and rubbed his hands, and remarked that Rand seemed to have been a mysterious chap—only had his flat a few weeks, not used it regularly, not by any means; no visitors to speak of, civil but distant. "That sounds all right," said Bell, and looked at Reggie.

"What was he like?" said Reggie.

"Middle size to biggish, wore glasses, well dressed, brown hair, which he wore rather long, they say," the inspector reeled off glibly.

"That's put the lid on," said Bell. "Won't do for the corpse. Warren. Not a bit like it. Well, sir, where are we now?" He turned to Reggie.

"You will go so fast," Reggie complained, and sat down. "I'm pantin' after you in vain. What's the primary hypothesis, Bell?"

"Sir?"

"Do we assume the corpse is Rand, or that Rand chucked the corpse out of window?"

"Ah, there's that," said the inspector eagerly. "We hadn't worked on that."

"We haven't worked on anything, if you ask me," said Bell gloomily. "What's your opinion then, Mr. Fortune?"

"The primary hypothesis is that we're looking for an able, masterful madman. Therefore my opinion is that the whole thing will look perfectly rational when we've got it all combed out—grantin' the madman's original mad idea."

"Am I to go round London looking for a rational madman?" Bell protested.

"My dear chap, you could catch 'em by the thousand. There's nobody so damned rational as the lunatic. That's where he falls down. Do not be discouraged. He's logical. He don't keep his eye on the facts. That is where we come in."

"We've come in all right, but we don't seem like getting out," Bell grumbled. "I'm keeping my eye on the facts all right. But they won't fit."

"You're very hasty to-day, Bell," said Reggie mildly. "Why is this?"

"I can see that fellow's face," Bell muttered.

"Well, well! He's told us all he can, poor devil. We'll get on, if you please. Because Rand's away, it don't follow that Rand's the corpse. It might have come out of some other tenant's window. Know anything about the other tenants?"

"All most respectable, sir," said the inspector.

"My dear man, the whole affair is most respectable. Do get that into your head. I dare say we'll find the corpse was a conveyancer murdered by a civil servant. A crime of quiet middle-class taste. What sort of fellows are the other fellows?"

"Well, sir, there's a retired engineer, and a young chap, just married, in the Rimington firm, and a naval officer, and several young doctors with consulting-rooms in Harley Street, and one of the Maynards, the Devonshire family. That's all with any rooms on the well. I've seen 'em all, and, if you ask me, they're right out of it; they're not the sort, not one of them."

"I dare say," said Reggie. "They don't sound as if they would fit. None of them heard anything?"

"No, sir; that's queer, to be sure."

"It happened the night of the blizzard. You wouldn't have noticed a bomb. Well, who was Rand?"

"That's what no one knows, sir. He'd only been here a few weeks. They're service flats, you know, and furnished. He gave a banker's reference. Bank says he has no money reason to be missing. Quiet, stable account. Income from investments. Balance three hundred odd. But the bank don't know anything about him. He's had an account for years. He used to live off Jermyn Street, apartment-house. The landlady died last year."

"And the landlady died last year," Reggie repeated. "He's elusive, is Mr. Rand. Same like our corpse. But is Rand missing, Bell? He's not been seen for a few days. There's not much in that. He never used his flat regularly."

"And, so far as we know, deceased isn't Rand."

"Well, I don't know quite as far as that," said Reggie.

"Good Lord, the porter who found him didn't recognize the body."

"Remember his face."

"My God, don't talk about his face."

"Sorry, sorry. Well, I dare say the porter was upset too."

"Yes, but the porter said Rand was biggish, and the body's on the small side. The porter said he had a lot of hair, and the body's absolutely bald."

"My dear chap, give a man a straight back and a bit of manner and lots of fellows think he's biggish—while he's alive. And a man that's absolutely bald is just the man to wear a wig."

"I thought we were to go by facts," Bell said gloomily.

"And so we are, Bell. Just a-going to begin, Mr. Snodgrass, sir. No rash haste."

"Have you got something up your sleeve?"

"Not one little trump. Oh, my dear Bell, how can you? Did I ever? My simple open heart is broken."

"You're damned cheerful, aren't you?"

"My dear man, I never made you swear before. My dear Bell! Sorry. Let's get on. Let's get on. I want to call on the elusive Rand."

There was nothing individual about the rooms of Mr. Rand. He had been content with the furniture supplied by the owners of the place, which was of the usual wholesale dullness. Reggie turned to the manager of the flats. "I suppose there's nothing in the place Mr. Rand owns? Not even the pictures?"

"The pictures were supplied by the contractors for the furniture, sir. So — —"

"The Lord have mercy on their souls," said Reggie.

"So there is nothing of the tenant's personal property except his clothes."

"He is elusive, our friend Rand," Reggie murmured, wandering about the room. "Smoked rather a showy cigar. Drank a fair whisky. Doesn't tell us much about him. Do the servants come here every day?"

The manager was embarrassed. "Well, sir, in point of fact, we're short-handed just now. Not unless they're rung for. Not unless we know the tenant's using the rooms."

"Don't apologize, don't apologize. In point of fact, they haven't been here since" — he looked critically at some dust upon a grim bronze — "since when?"

"I should say some days," said the manager, with diffidence.

"I should say a week. No matter. Many thanks."

Superintendent Bell with some urgency ushered the manager out. When he had done that he turned upon his inspector. "Confound you. Warren, what do you want to stare at the waste-paper basket for? That chap would have seen it if Mr. Fortune hadn't got interested in the smokes and drinks."

Reggie laughed and the inspector abased himself. "Very sorry, sir. Didn't know I stared. But it is so blooming odd."

Bell snorted and lifted the basket on to the table. It was nearly full of black burnt paper. "Why did they burn it in the basket?" said the inspector.

"Because the fireplaces are all gas stoves, I suppose," said Bell. "But I don't know why they couldn't leave the stuff on the hearth."

"Because this is a tidy crime," said Reggie. "Nice, quiet, middle-class crime. No ugly mess. I told you that."

The Superintendent gazed at him. "Now what can you know, you know?"

"I don't know. I feel. I feel the kind of man that did it. Don't you? I'll lay you odds he came of a neat, virtuous, middle-class home."

The Superintendent started. "Who are you thinking of?"

"You are so hasty to-day. Bell. I haven't got a 'who'. Still anonymous is the slayer. But I'll swear I've got his character."

"Have you, though!" said Bell. "Tidy fellow! Don't make a mess! Remember that face?"

"Oh, I said he was mad."

"Well, I'm not yet. I'm only feeling what I can feel." He began to examine the burnt paper. "Letters mostly. Some stoutish paper. Some stuff looks a bit like a notebook. That's all we'll get out of that."

"Well, except the one thing. Whoever did that was clearing up. Clearing up something that might have left traces that might have been dangerous. Same like he cleared up the dead man's face. Don't you see? Somebody and some affair had to be absolutely abolished."

"Yes. What was it?"

"We mayn't ever know that," said Reggie slowly.

"I believe you," said Bell, and laughed. "I feel that, sir."

The inspector and he began to examine the room in detail, opening drawers and cupboards. But except for tobacco and spirits they found no trace of Mr. Rand. Nothing had been broken open, but nothing was locked. "No keys on the deceased, were there, Mr. Fortune?" said Bell suddenly. "And that's a point, too. Very few men go about without any keys."

"Well, hang it, very few men go about without any money," Reggie expostulated. "The corpse hadn't a copper. You can take it the way we found him wasn't the way he used to go about. He'd do his vest up, for instance."

"Ah," said Bell sagely. "You've got it all in your head, I must say. That's the thing about you, Mr. Fortune, if you don't mind my saying so. You've always got a whole case in your mind at once; there's some of us only see it in bits, so to speak."

123

Reggie smiled. He understood that Superintendent Bell was repenting of having lost his temper, and was anxious to make it up. "I never found so good a fellow to work with as you. Bell," he said. "You always keep a level head."

Superintendent Bell shook it and stared at Reggie. "Not to-day. As you know very well, Mr. Fortune, begging your pardon. I've been rattled, and that's the truth. Ought to know better at my time of life, to be sure. I've seen a good deal, too, you might say. But there's some things I'll never get used to. And that chap's face upset me."

Reggie nodded. "Yes. I was sayin' — the only things that make you afraid are the mad things. And the only thing that does you good is to fight 'em. That's why I've cheered up."

"That's right, sir. Well, now, these facts of yours. There's no papers anywhere. All burnt in that basket. Rather odd there is not so much as a book."

"I don't think he was a man of culture, the elusive Rand. But you've missed something, haven't you?"

"I dare say," Bell grinned. "I generally do when you're about."

"There's not a sign the murder was done in this room."

"Oh, I saw that all right. But we hadn't any reason to think it was."

"No," Reggie sighed, "No. So tidy. So tidy." And they went into Mr. Rand's bedroom.

That also was tidy. No trace of a struggle, of blood. That also had no papers, no books, nothing personal but clothes.

"Spent a good deal at his tailor's," said Bell, looking into a well-filled wardrobe, and read out the name of a man in Savile Row. "Hallo. They're not all the same make. Some cheaper stuff. Why, what's the matter with his boots, sir?" For Reggie was taking up one pair after another.

"Nothing. All quite satisfactory. About a nine and rather broad. The corpse wore about a nine and had a broad foot. What's that about his clothes? Different tailors? Are the clothes all the same size? All made for the same man?" Suit after suit was spread out on the bed. They were to the same measure; they all were marked "W. H. Rand". "Quite satisfactory," Reggie purred. "They'd fit the corpse all right. Pretty different styles, though. He dressed to look different at different times. He is elusive, is W. H. Rand."

They began to open drawers. There was the same abundance, the same variety of styles in Mr. Rand's hosiery. "Yes, he meant to be elusive," Reggie murmured. "Anything from a bookmaker to a churchwarden at a funeral. 16½ collars, though. And that's the measure of the corpse. Is all the linen marked?"

It was, and with ink, so that the mark could only be removed by taking out a piece of the stuff. "If the corpse is Rand, where the devil did his shirt come from?" said Reggie. "The slayer unpicked the name from his coat. That was one of the Savile Row suits. But the shirt? Did the slayer bring a change of linen with him? Provident fellow, very provident."

Bell, on his knees by a chest of drawers, gave a grunt. "Lord, here's a drawer tumbled. And that's the first yet. It's new stuff, too—not worn."

Reggie bent over him and whistled. "Not marked. Same sort of stuff as the corpse wears. And the drawer's left untidy. The first untidy drawer. Well, well. Everybody breaks down somewhere. He began to be untidy then. When he got to the shirt and the vest." He shivered and turned away to the window. "This damned place looks out on the well," he cried out, and turned back and sat down. "Bah! The slayer did that, I suppose," he muttered, and sprang up. "Believe in ghosts, you men?"

"Good Lord, sir, don't you start giving us the jumps!" said Bell.

Reggie was at the dressing-table. "Sorry, sorry," he said over his shoulder, opening and shutting drawers. Then he turned with something in his hands. "That wasn't such a bad shot of mine. Bell. Here's a wig. The corpse is uncommon bald. The elusive Rand had lots of brown hair. Here's a nice brown wig."

"There's no blood on it!" Bell cried.

"No. I guess this is Mr. Rand's second best. The one he had on when he was killed wouldn't look nice now."

"That about settles it," Bell said slowly.

"We haven't seen the bathroom," said Reggie.

Bell looked at him and shrugged.

"Not likely to be much there, sir," said the inspector.

"There could be," said Reggie gravely, and led the way.

It was a bathroom of some size but no luxury. Only the sheer necessities of bathing were provided. The lower half of the walls was tiled, the floor of linoleum. Reggie stopped in the doorway. "Anything strike you about it, Bell?"

"Looks new, sir."

"Yes. Nice and clean. Tidy, don't you know. But there's no towels and no sponge. Yet in the bedroom everything was ready for Rand to sleep there to-night—pyjamas, brushes and comb, everything. Didn't he use towels? Didn't he have a sponge?"

"What do you mean, sir?"

"This is where the slayer cleared up after the murder. And he took the dirty towels and the bloody sponge away with him. Tidy fellow—always tidy. Just wait, will you?" And he went into the bathroom on all fours. About the middle of the room he stopped, and pored over the linoleum, and felt it with the tips of his fingers. Then he stood up and went to the window, opened it, and looked out. He examined the sill, and then sat himself on it in the manner of a window cleaner, and began to study the window frame. After a minute or two he pulled out a pocket-knife, and with great care cut a piece of wood. He put this down on the edge of the porcelain basin, and resumed his study. When he had finished he went down again on his hands and knees, and wandered over the floor. He made an exclamation, he lay down on his stomach, and stretched underneath the bath. When he stood up he had in his hand something that glittered. He held it out on his palm to Bell.

"What's that, sir? A match-box?"

"It might be. A gold match-box—provisionally. No name. No initials. On opening—we find inside—a little white powder"—he smelt it, put a fragment on the tip of his finger and tasted—"which is cocaine. Well, come in, Bell, come in. See what you can make of the place. I can't find a finger-print anywhere." He slipped the gold box into his pocket.

The two detectives came in, and went over the room even more minutely than he. "There's nothing that tells me anything," said Bell.

Reggie sat on the edge of the bath. "Well, well, I wouldn't say that," he said mildly. "It's not what we could wish, Bell. But there are points—there are points."

"All right, sir. Call Mr. Fortune," Bell grinned.

"I don't say it'll ever go into court. But some things we do know. The dead man is Rand, the elusive Rand. He had papers worth burning. He

126

was killed by a powerful man with one or two blows, probably in the sitting-room. After death he was stripped and dressed in the unmarked clothes, probably here. For his body was brought where a mess could be cleaned up, to have the face smashed in. You can see the dents in the linoleum where his head lay. And then he was pitched out by that window. There's a bit of animal matter, probably human tissue, on that scrap of wood. Then the slayer packed up everything that was bloody and went off; and one of 'em — the tidy slayer or the elusive Rand — one of 'em used cocaine."

Superintendent Bell shrugged his shoulders. "It don't take us very far, sir, does it? It don't amount to so much. What I should call a baffling case. I mean to say, we don't seem to get near anybody."

Reggie grunted, got off the bath, and taking with him his bit of wood, went back to the sitting-room, the two detectives in silent attendance. There he tumbled Mr. Rand's cigarettes out of their box, and put his bit of wood in it.

"I suppose there's nothing more here," he murmured, his eyes wandering round the room. "Try it with the lights on. Switch on, inspector. . . . No. Ah, what's that?" He went to the gas fire and picked out of its lumps of sham coal a scrap of gleaming metal. The next moment he was down on his knees, pulling the fire to pieces. "Give me an envelope, will you?" he said over his shoulder, and they saw he was collecting scraps of broken glass.

"What is it, sir?"

"That's the bridge of a pair of rimless eyeglasses. And if we're lucky we can reconstruct the lenses. When Rand was hit, his glasses jumped off and smashed themselves. That's the fourth thing the slayer didn't think of."

"You don't miss much, Mr. Fortune. Still, it is baffling, very baffling. Even now, we don't know anybody, so to speak. We don't even know Rand. What was Rand, would you say? It was worth somebody's while to do him in. I suppose he knew something. But what did he know? Who was Rand?"

Reggie was putting on his overcoat. He collected his envelope and his cigarette box and put them away, looking the while with dreamy eyes at Superintendent Bell. "Yes," he said; "yes, there's a lot of unknown quantities about just now. Who the devil was Rand? Well, well! I think that finishes us here. Will you ring for the lift, inspector?" When he was left alone with Bell, he still gazed dreamily at that plump, stolid face. "Yes. Who the devil was Rand? And if you come to that, who the devil is Sandford?"

"Good Lord, Mr. Fortune, do you mean this business is that business?"

"Well, there's a lot of unknown quantities about," said Reggie.

Phase IV.—The Charge

When they talked about the case afterwards, Reggie and Lomas used to agree that it was a piece of pure art. "Crime unstained by any vulgar greed or sentiment; sheer crime; iniquity neat. An impressive thing, Lomas, old dear."

"So it is," Lomas nodded. "One meets cases of the kind, but never quite of so pure a style. Upon my soul, Fortune, it has a sort of grandeur — the intensity of purpose, the contempt for ordinary values, the absolute uselessness of it. And it was damned clever."

Reggie chose a cigar. "Great work," he sighed. "All the marks of the real great man, if it wasn't diabolical. He was a great man, but for the hate in him. Just like the devil."

"You're so moral," Lomas protested. "Don't you feel the beauty of it?"

"Of course I'm moral. I'm sane. Oh, so sane, Lomas, old thing. That's why I beat the wily criminal. And the devil, God help him."

"Yes, you're as sane as a boy," Lomas nodded.

But all that was afterwards.

Everything that was done in the case is not (though you may have feared so) written here. We take it in the critical, significant scenes, and the next of them arrived some days after the discovery of the corpse.

Lomas was in his room with Superintendent Bell, when Kimball came to them. He was brisker than ever. "Anything new, is there? Have you hit on anything? I came round at once, you see, when I got your note. Delighted to get it. Much better to have all the details cleared up. Well, what is it?"

"I'm afraid I've nothing for you myself," said Lomas. "The fact is, Fortune thought you might be able to give him some information on one or two points."

"I? God bless me, you know all that I know. Where is he, then, if he wants me?"

And Reggie came. "Have you been waitin'?" he said, with his airiest manner. "So sorry. Things are really rollin' up, you know. New facts by every post. Well, well." He dropped into a chair and blinked at the party.

"What are we all doin' here? Oh, ah! I remember." He smiled and nodded at Kimball. "It was that fellow I wanted to ask you about."

Kimball, as was natural, did not relish this sort of thing. "I understood you had something important on hand. I've no time to waste."

"Why, it's so jolly hard to understand what's important and what isn't, don't you know? But it all comes out in the end."

"You think so, do you? This is the coal affair?"

"I wouldn't say that," Reggie answered thoughtfully. "No, I wouldn't say that. After all, the Coal Ramp isn't the only pebble on the beach."

"Then why the devil do you bother me?" Kimball cried.

Reggie sat up suddenly. "Because this is something you must know." He rearranged his coat and slid down into the chair again, and drawled out what he had to say. "Some time the end of last year—point of fact—last December—bein' quite precise, from fifth to twenty-ninth—in one of the nursin'-homes in Queen Anne Street—speakin' strictly, No. 1003—there was a man bein' operated on by Sir Jenkin Totteridge for an affection of the middle ear. This chap was called Mason. You went to see him several times. Who was Mason?"

Kimball stared at him with singular intensity. Then he swung half round in his chair with one of his characteristic jerky movements, and pulled out his snuffbox. He took a pinch. "You've found a mare's nest," he said, with a laugh, and took another pinch.

As he spoke, Reggie sprang up with some vehemence, bumping into his arm. "Sorry—sorry. A mare's nest, you say? Now what exactly do you mean by that?"

Kimball stood up too. "I mean you're wasting my time," he said.

"That isn't what I should call an explanation," Reggie murmured. "For instance, do you mean you didn't go to see Mason?"

"Don't let's have any more of this damned trifling," Kimball cried. "Certainly I went to see Mason."

"Good! Who is he?"

"Jack Mason is a fellow I knew in my early days. I went up and he didn't. I've seen little of him this ten years. When he had that operation, poor chap, he wrote to me, and I went to see him for the sake of old times. And what the devil has it to do with Scotland Yard?"

"Mason is the man who was found at the Montmorency House flats with his face smashed in."

"God bless my soul! Mason! Poor chap, poor chap! But what are you talking about? The papers said that was a man called Rand."

"Mason, otherwise Rand. Rand, otherwise Mason. Who was Mason, and why did somebody kill him?"

Kimball made one of his jerky gestures. "Killed, was he? I thought he fell out of the window."

"He was murdered."

"Good God! Old Jack Mason! It's beyond me. I haven't a notion. You know this upsets me a good deal. I've seen little of him for a long time. I can hardly believe he's gone. But why the devil did he call himself Rand?"

"What was he?" said Reggie sharply.

"God bless me, I couldn't tell you," Kimball laughed. "He was always very close. An agent in a small way, when I knew him — colonial produce, and so forth. I fancy he went in for building land. Comfortably off always, but he never got on. Very reserved fellow. Loved to be mysterious. No. I suppose it isn't surprising he used two names."

"Why was he murdered?" said Reggie.

"I can't help you."

"That's all you can say?"

"Yes. Afraid so. Yes. Let me know as soon as you have anything more. Good morning, good morning." He bustled out.

"A bit hurried, as you might say," said Superintendent Bell.

Reggie picked up a paper-knife and fell on his knees. He rose with some fragments of white powder on the blade. "I suppose you saw me jog his arm," he said. "And that's cocaine." He tumbled Lomas's paper-clips out of their box and put the stuff in. "Do you remember the first time we had him here, he took snuff? I thought he was rather odd about it and after it, and I went over to the window where he stood to see if I could find any of the stuff he used. But he'd been careful. He is careful, is Kimball."

"He is damned careful," Lomas agreed, and began to write on a scribbling-pad, looking at each word critically.

There was a pause. "Beg your pardon, sir," said Superintendent Bell. "You talked about the murder being a madman's job. Do you mean Mr. Kimball, being a dope fiend, is not responsible for his actions?"

"O Lord, no. Kimball's not a dope fiend. He uses the stuff same like we use whisky. He's not a slave to it yet. Say he's a heavy drinker. It's just beginnin' to interfere with his efficiency. That's why he left the box behind in the bathroom; that's why he's a little jerky. But he's pretty adequate still."

"You talked about mad. You were emphatic, as you might say," Bell insisted. "What might you have in your mind, sir? Mr. Kimball's generally reckoned uncommon practical."

"He isn't ordinary mad," said Reggie. "He don't think he's Julius Cæsar or a poached egg. He don't go out without his trousers. He don't see red and go it blind. But there is something queer in him. I doubt if they're physical, these perversions. Call it a disease of the soul."

"Ah, well, his soul," said Bell gravely. "I judge he's not a Christian man."

"I wish I did know his creed," said Reggie, with equal gravity. "It would be very instructive."

Lomas tapped his pencil impatiently. "We're not evangelists, we're policemen," he said. "And what do we do next?"

"Take out a warrant and arrest Kimball," said Reggie carelessly.

Bell and Lomas looked at each other and then at him. "I don't see my way," said Lomas.

"The corpse can be identified as Mason. I'll swear to the operation. Totteridge will swear it's the man he operated on as Mason. Kimball admits several visits to Mason. In the room from which the corpse was thrown was a gold snuff-box containing cocaine. Shortman's will swear that box is their make and exactly similar to a box sold to Kimball. And Kimball takes cocaine. It's a good prima facie case."

"Yes. Did you ever see a jury that would hang a man on it?"

"We do have to be so careful," Bell murmured.

Reggie laughed. "And Kimball's a Cabinet Minister."

"Damn it. Fortune, be fair!" Lomas cried. "If I had a sound case against a man, he would stand his trial whoever he was. I don't wink at a fellow who's got a pull. You know that. But there's a reason in all things. I can't charge a Cabinet Minister with murder on evidence like this. What is it after all?" He picked up his scribbling-pad and read: 'Three circumstances—Kimball knew the murdered man; a snuff-box like

Kimball's was found on the scene of the murder; that snuff-box held cocaine, and cocaine is what Kimball uses.' Circumstantial evidence at its weakest. Neither judge nor jury would look at it. There's no motive, there's no explanation of the method of the crime. My dear chap, suppose you were on the other side, you'd tear it to ribbons in five minutes."

"On the other side?" Reggie repeated slowly. "I'm not an advocate, Lomas. I'm always on the same side. I'm for justice. I'm for the man who's been wronged."

Lomas stared at him. "Yes. Quite—quite. But we generally take all that for granted, don't we? My dear chap, you mustn't mind my saying so, but you do preach a good deal over this case."

"I had noticed the same thing myself," said Superintendent Bell, and they both looked curiously at Reggie.

"Why am I so moral? Because the thing's so damned immoral," said Reggie vehemently. "What's most crime? Human. Human greed, human lust, human hostility. But this is diabolical. Sheer evil for evil's sake. Lomas, I'll swear, when we have it all out, we'll find that it still looks unreasonable, futile, pure passion for wrong."

"Meaning Mr. Kimball mad. You do come back to that, sir," Bell said.

"Not legally mad. Probably not medically mad. I mean he has the devil in him."

"Really, my dear Fortune, you do surprise me," Lomas said. "I perceive that in all things you are too superstitious. The right honourable gentleman hath a devil! It isn't done, you know. This is the twentieth century. And you're a scientific man. Consider your reputation—and mine, if you don't mind. What the devil are we to do? Try exorcism?"

"You won't charge Kimball?" Lomas signified an impatient negative. "Very well. You say you don't let a man off because he's in the Government. Suppose you had a prima facie case like this against a nobody. Suppose I brought you as good grounds for arresting Sandford. Wouldn't you have him in the dock? On your conscience now!"

Again Bell and Lomas consulted each other's faces. "I wonder why you drag in Sandford?" said Lomas slowly.

"He's in it all right. I asked you a question."

"Well, if you insist. One might charge a man on a prima facie case, to hear his defence."

133

Reggie struck his hand on the table. "There it is! A man who is nobody — he can stand trial. Not a Cabinet Minister. Oh dear, no!"

"My dear fellow, the world is what it is. You know very well that if I wanted to charge Kimball on this evidence it would be turned down. I couldn't force the issue without a stronger case. Do have some sense of the practical."

Reggie smiled. "I'm not blaming you. I only want to rub it in."

"Thanks very much. We are to suspect Kimball, I suppose."

"Like the devil, and watch him."

"I see. Yes, I think we shall be quite justified in watching Mr. Kimball. But, my dear fellow, you are rather odd this morning. If you want Kimball watched, why the devil do you handle him so violently? You know, you almost accused him of the murder. Anything more likely to put him on his guard I can't imagine."

"Yes, yes. I think I made him jump," said Reggie, with satisfaction. "Quite intentional, Lomas, old thing. He's on his guard all right. But he don't know how little we know. I meant to put him in a funk. I want to see what a funk will make him do."

Lomas looked at him steadily. "For a very moral man," he said, "you have a good deal of the devil about you."

"I think I ought to say, Mr. Fortune," said Bell, "we've all been in a hurry to judge Mr. Kimball. I said things myself. And I do say he's not a Christian man — an unbeliever, I'm afraid. But I ought to say too, he lives a very clean life. Always has. Temperate, very quiet style, a thorough good master, generous to his employees, and always ready to come down handsome for a good cause."

"Who is Kimball, Bell?" said Reggie quietly.

"Sir?" Bell stared. "He's always been known, sir. Started in Liverpool on the Cotton Exchange. Went into rubber. Came to London. That's his career. All quite open and straight."

"And we don't know a damned thing about him."

"Well, really, Fortune, you're rather exacting. You're after his soul, I suppose," said Lomas, with something like a sneer.

"Who is Kimball?" Reggie insisted. "There's two unknown quantities. Who is Kimball? Who is Sandford?"

"I'm afraid you want the Day of Judgment, my dear fellow," said Lomas. "'Unto whom all hearts are open, all desires known' — that sort of thing. Well, we can't ring up the Recording Angel from here. It's a trunk call."

"I know you're worldly. But you might know your world. Look about, Lomas, old thing. I've been looking about." He took out a newspaper cutting.

Lomas read: "'SANDFORD. Anyone who can give any information about Mrs. Ellen Edith Sandford, resident Llanfairfechan from 1882-1900, formerly of Lancashire, is urgently begged to communicate with XYZ.'" He looked up. "Of Lancashire? That's a guess?"

Reggie nodded. "North Wales is mostly Lancashire people."

"Well, there's no harm in it. Do you want us to advertise for Kimball's wet nurse?"

"And his sisters and his cousins and his aunts. Yes. All in good time. But watch him first. Watch them both." He nodded, and sauntered out.

Lomas lit a cigarette and pushed the box to Bell. Both men smoked a minute in silence. Then Lomas said, "That's a damned clever fellow. Bell."

"Yes, sir."

"I've often thought he was too clever by half. But, damme, I don't remember thinking he was uncanny before."

"I have noticed it," said Bell diffidently, "in a manner of speaking. Of course he does know a lot, does Mr. Fortune, a rare lot of stuff. But that's natural, as were. What upsets you is the sort of way he feels men. It's as if he had senses you haven't got. Very strange the way he knows men."

Phase V.—The Reply

Their admiration for Reggie Fortune received a shock the next day. It came by telephone. Just after his late and lazy breakfast, Reggie was rung up from Scotland Yard. Bell spoke. Mr. Lomas thought that Mr. Fortune would like to know that Sandford had gone down to Mr. Kimball's place. Reggie answered, "Oh, Peter!" In a quarter of an hour he was in Lomas's room asking for confirmation. There was no doubt. The detective watching Sandford's chambers had followed him to Victoria, and heard him take a ticket to Alwynstow, Kimball's place, and was gone with him.

"So that's the next move," said Lomas, "and if you can tell me what it means I shall be obliged to you."

Reggie dropped his hand on the table. "Not a guess," he said. "How can a man guess? We don't even know how much they know, or whether one knows what the other knows. I could fancy Sandford—what's the use?

"'So runs my dream. But what am I?
An infant crying in the night,
An infant crying for the light,
And with no language but a cry.'

Same like you, Lomas."

"I notice you are not so much the moral sage this morning," Lomas said sourly.

"Lomas, dear, don't be unkind. I can't bear it. I wish to God I was down there!"

"Damn it, we've got two men down there now—one on Sandford, one on Kimball. They'll be knocking their heads together. What the devil do you think you could do?"

"Nothing. Lord, don't I know it? Nothing. That's what makes me peevish."

Lomas said severely that he had work to do, and Reggie left him, promising to come back and take him out to lunch, which he received as if it were a threat.

But when Reggie did come back, Superintendent Bell was in the room and Lomas listening to the telephone. Bell looked oddly at Reggie. Lomas raised a blank and pallid face from the receiver. "Sandford has murdered Kimball," he said.

"Oh, Peter! I wonder if he's brought it off," Reggie murmured. "Has he brought it off after all?" He bit his lip. Lomas was talking into the telephone. Asking for details, giving instructions. "Hold the line. Cut that out," said Reggie. "We'll go down, Lomas, please. Tell your chap to meet us at the house. My car's here."

Lomas gave the orders and rang off. "I'll have to go, I suppose," he agreed. "One doesn't kill Cabinet Ministers every day. More's the pity. Damn the case! There's nothing in it, though, Fortune. Sandford was walking up to the house. He met Kimball in the lane. They were crossing the ornamental water in the park when they had a quarrel. Kimball was thrown in. He called out, "You scoundrel, you have murdered me." When they got Kimball out he was dead. That's all. I'm afraid it washes your stuff about Kimball right out."

"Well, well," Reggie drawled, looking through his eyelashes. "Where is he that knows, Lomas? From the great deep to the great deep he goes, Lomas. We'll get on."

"What about lunch?"

"Damn lunch!" said Reggie, and went out.

The other two, who liked food far less than he but could not go without it, lingered to collect sandwiches, and found him chafing in the driver's seat.

They exchanged looks of horror. "I'm too old for Mr. Fortune's driving, and that's a fact," Bell mumbled.

"When I got out alive after that day at Woking I swore I'd never go again," said Lomas.

But they quailed before Reggie's virulent politeness when he asked them if they would please get in. . . . It is in the evidence of Lomas that they only slowed once, when an old lady dropped her handkerchief in the middle of Croydon. He is in conflict with the statement of Bell as to the most awful moment. For he selects the episode of the traction-engine with trucks at the Alwynstow cross-roads, and Bell chooses the affair of the motor-bus and the caravan at Merstham. They agree that they arrived at Alwynstow Park in a cold sweat.

A detective came out on the steps to meet them, and watched reverently Bell and Lomas helping each other out. Reggie ran up to him. "Which are you?"

"Beg pardon, sir? Oh, I'm Hall. I had Mr. Kimball. It was Parker had Mr. Sandford." He turned to Lomas. "Good morning, sir. I tried to get you on the telephone, but they said you were on your way down."

"Oh, you've been on the telephone too?"

"When I heard what Parker's information was I rung up quick, sir. It's a very queer business, sir."

"Where is Parker? And where's Sandford? I suppose you've arrested him?"

"Well, no, sir. Not strictly speaking. We detained him pending instructions."

"Damme, you're very careful. Parker saw the murder committed, didn't he?"

"Well, sir, if I may say so, that's drawing conclusions. I don't understand Parker would go as far as that."

"Good Gad!" said Lomas. "Where the devil is Parker?"

"Keeping Mr. Sandford under observation, sir, according to instructions. Beg your pardon, sir. I've heard his story, and I quite agree it all happened like that. But you haven't heard mine."

Lomas looked round him. The house was too near. "We'll walk on the lawn," he announced. "Now then. Parker says the two men quarrelled on the bridge over the lake and Kimball was thrown in, and as he fell he called out, 'You scoundrel, you've murdered me!' And you say that isn't murder."

"Did Sergeant Parker say 'thrown in'?" said Hall, with surprise in his face and his voice.

"I believe he didn't," said Lomas slowly. "No. He said Kimball was thrown off, and as he fell in he called out."

"That's right, sir," said Hall heartily. "But I reckon there is more to it than that. When Mr. Kimball came out this morning I was waiting for him in the park. It was rather touch and go, because he had some men at work above the lake. He went down that way to the station. As he was crossing the bridge he tried the rails. It's very odd, sir, but a bit of the bar—it's a sort of rustic stuff—was that loose it came off in his hand. He put it back and went on. He met Mr. Sandford in the road and turned back with him. I had to get out of the way quick. I judged they were coming back to the house, so I did a run and dropped over the fence, and was away on the other side of the lake. Then I went into the rhododendrons and waited for them to pass. You see, sir, Parker had to keep well out of sight behind, and I was as near as makes no matter. Well, if you'll believe me, it was Mr. Kimball made the quarrel, and all in a minute he made it. One minute they were walking quite friendly, the next he whips round on Mr. Sandford and he called him a bad name. I couldn't hear all, he was talking so quick, but there was ugly words in it. Then he made to strike Mr. Sandford, and Mr. Sandford closed and chucked him back, and into the water he went just where that same rail that he looked at was loose. But it's true enough as he fell he called out, 'You scoundrel, you've murdered me!'"

"Well, well. So he didn't bring it off after all," said Reggie. "We trumped his last card."

"Sir?" said the detective.

"You were the trump," said Reggie. "Oh, my aunt, I feel much better! I wonder if there's any lunch in these parts. What about it, Lomas, old thing?"

"I'm damned if I understand," said Lomas. "I want Sandford. Let's go up to the house."

They found Sandford sitting in an easy-chair in the dead man's library. He was reading; to Reggie's ineffable admiration he was reading a book by Mr. Sidney Webb on the history of trade unions. Sergeant Parker, the detective, made himself uncomfortable at the table and pored over his notebook.

"All right, all right, Parker. Quite understood." Lomas waved him away. "Good afternoon, Mr. Sandford. Sorry to detain you. Most unfortunate affair."

"Good afternoon. It is not necessary to apologize," said Sandford, completely himself. "I realize that the police must require my account of the affair. Yesterday afternoon Mr. Kimball rang me up at my rooms. I did

139

not learn from where he was speaking. He said that my affair — that was his phrase — my affair had taken a new turn, and he wished me to come and see him here this morning. He named the train by which I was to travel. I thought it strange that he should bring me into the country, but I had no valid ground of objection. Accordingly I came this morning. I thought it strange that he sent no conveyance to meet me. I started to walk to the house. In the lane he met me walking. He talked of indifferent things in a rather broken manner, I thought, but that was common with him, and yet I was surprised he did not come to the point. He was, however, quite friendly until we reached the bridge over the lake. Then without any warning or reason he turned upon me and was violently abusive. His language was vulgar and even filthy. He attempted to strike me, and I defended myself. I was, in fact, a good deal alarmed, for he was, as you know, much bigger and heavier than I, and he was in a frenzy of rage. To my surprise, I may say my relief, I was able to resist him. I pushed him off — really, you know, it seemed quite easy — and the hand-rail behind him gave way and he fell into the water. As he fell he called out, 'You scoundrel, you have murdered me!' I can only suppose he was not responsible for his actions."

"Much obliged," said Lomas. "I'm afraid you've had a distressing time."

"It has been a remarkable experience," said Sandford. "May I ask if there is any reason why I should not return to town?"

"No, no." Lomas looked at him queerly. "You have an uncommon cool head. They'll want your evidence at the inquest, of course. But it's fair to say I quite accept your story."

"I am obliged to you," said Sandford, in a tone of surprise, as if he could not conceive that any one should not. "I am told there is a train at 3.35. Good afternoon."

"One moment. One moment," said Reggie. "Do you know of any reason in the world Kimball had to hate you?"

"Certainly not," said Sandford, in offended dignity. "Our relations were short and wholly official. I conceive that he had no reason to complain of my services."

"And yet he meant to murder you or have you hanged for his murder."

"If he did, I can only suppose that he was out of his mind."

140

"Was he out of his mind when he worked the Coal Ramp to ruin you?"

"Dear me," said Sandford, "do you really suggest, sir, that Mr. Kimball was responsible for that scandalous piece of finance?"

"Who else?"

"But really—you startle me. That is to say, as a Minister he betrayed the secrets of the department?"

"Well, he didn't stick at a trifle, did he?"

"The poor fellow must have been mad," said Sandford, with grave sympathy.

"Yes, yes. But why was he mad? Why did he hate you? My dear chap, do search your memory. Can you think of any sort of connection between Kimball and you?"

"I never heard of him till he became prominent in the House. I never saw him till he came into the office. Our relations were always perfectly correct. No, I can only suppose that he was insane. Is it any use to try to discover reasons for the antipathies of madness? I have not studied the subject, but it seems obvious that they must be irrational. I am sorry I cannot help your investigations. I believe I had better catch my train. Good afternoon."

"You know, I begin to like that fellow. He's so damned honest," said Reggie.

"Cold-blooded fish," said Lomas. "Begad, he don't know how near he was to dead. Did you ever hear anything less plausible than that yarn of his? If we didn't know it was true we wouldn't believe a word of it. Good God, suppose Hall hadn't been down here watching! We should have had the outside facts. Sandford, who had been accused and suspended by Kimball, suddenly comes down to Kimball's house, meets him, quarrels with him, and throws him into the lake."

"And the men working in the park a little way off just saw the struggle, just heard Kimball call out that he was murdered," said Reggie. "Don't forget the men. They're a most interesting touch. He always thought of everything, did Mr. Kimball. He had them there, just the right distance for the evidence he wanted. I don't know if you see the full significance of those men working in the park."

Lomas sat down. "I don't mind owning I thought they were accidental."

"My dear chap! Oh, my dear chap, there was very little accidental in the vicinity of the late Kimball. They were there to give evidence that would hang Sandford. And that proves Kimball didn't mean to throw Sandford into the lake. He wanted to be thrown in, he wanted to be killed, and get Sandford hanged for it."

"I suppose so," Lomas agreed. "It's a case that's happened before. And you couldn't always say the creatures that planned it were mad."

"Not legally mad. Not medically mad. I always said that. No, I don't know that it's even very strange. Quite a lot of people would be ready to die if they could get their enemies killed by their death. Only they don't see their way. But he was an able fellow, the late Kimball."

"Able! I should say so. If our men hadn't been here, Sandford would have been as good as hanged. Nobody could have believed his story. Why did he come here? There could be no evidence of Kimball's telephone call. What did Sandford come for? There's no reasonable reason. Kimball put him under a cloud, he was furious, he meant murder, and did it. The jury wouldn't leave the box."

"That's right, sir," said Superintendent Bell. "If it wasn't for Mr. Fortune he'd be down and out. What you might call a rarity in our work, that is, to save a man from a charge of murder before it comes along."

"How do you mean?" Reggie seemed to come back from other thoughts. "Oh, because I told you to have Kimball watched. Well, it was pretty clear he wasn't the kind to go about without a chaperon. We took that trick. I suppose Kimball's thinking, wherever he is, that we won the game. But I wouldn't say that—I wouldn't say that. Why did he hate Sandford?"

"My dear fellow, the man was mad."

"You mean he didn't like the way Sandford does his hair—or he thought Sandford was a German spy. No. He wasn't that kind of mad. There's something we don't know, Lomas, old thing. I dare say it's crazy enough. I'll bet you my favourite shirt it's something the ordinary sane man feels."

"If we are to go looking for something crazy which sane men feel!" said Lomas.

"Speakin' broadly, all the human emotions," said Reggie. "Didn't you ever hate a man because he married a girl who was pretty? Don't be so godlike."

"They weren't either of them married, sir," said Bell, in grave surprise.

"How do you know?" Reggie snapped. "No, I don't suppose they were. But we don't know. We don't know anything. That's why I say we haven't won the game. Well, well. For God's sake let's have some food! There was a modest pub in the village. I saw it when you let off your futile scream at the traction-engine. Let's go. I don't seem to want to eat Kimball's grub."

Phase VI.—Jane Brown

Two or three days after Lomas received an invitation to lunch in Wimpole Street.

"I owe you one," Reggie wrote. "I owe myself one. I want to forget the high tea of Alwynstow. Do you remember the pickles? And the bacon? What had that pig been doing? A neurasthenic, I fear. A student of the Nematoda."

So naturally when Lomas came his first question was what Nematoda may be.

"Never mind," Reggie sighed. "It's a painful subject. A disgusting subject. Same like what we make our living by. They are among the criminals of animal life. Real bad eggs. A sad world, Lomas, old thing. Let's forget all about crime."

They did. For an hour and a half. At the end of which Lomas said dreamily, "You're a remarkable fellow, Fortune. I don't know how you can retain any brain. You do yourself so well. Yes, most seductive habit of life. I meant to say something when I came. What was it? I believe you have talked of everything else in creation. Ah, yes, did you ever hear of the Kimball case? Well, I think we have combed it all out."

"Have you, though?" Reggie sat up.

"Yes. We've been dealing with a stockbroker or two. I'm really afraid there was a little bullying. We hinted that there might be developments about a certain murder case. And two of them began to talk. We've got Rand-Mason's past."

"Oh, that!" Reggie said. "Quite obvious, wasn't it? Kimball meant to use this coal scheme to ruin Sandford. He sent Mason, who had probably been his go-between in other financial things, to give the brokers the tip. It was also Rand-Mason who paid the money into Sandford's account. Remember the stout man in glasses. Then probably he struck for better pay or they had a row. Anyway, he threatened to give the show away. Kimball couldn't trust him anymore. Daren't trust him. So he wiped Rand-Mason out. Is that right, sir?"

"I'm not omniscient myself. But certainly Rand-Mason was the man who put the brokers on to it. There is not much doubt he went to Sandford's bank. By the way, Kimball had several big sticks. His valet says he liked weight."

"I dare say. Had Kimball any papers?"

"Not a line that throws light on this. As you know everything, I'd like to hear why Kimball tried this murder plan last instead of first?"

"How can you be so unkind, Lomas? I keep telling you I don't know anything. I come and shout it in your ear. I don't know the thing that really matters. Who was Kimball? Who is Sandford? What is he that Kimball couldn't bear him? I said that at the beginning. I say it now in italics. Good Lord, you can hear Kimball laughing at us!"

"Don't be uncanny."

"Well, I'm not really sure he is laughing at us. Wait a while. But why did Kimball try murder last instead of first? Oh, that's easy. He was an epicure in hate! He didn't want mere blood. He wanted the beggar to suffer—to be ruined, not just dead. Hence he went to break Sandford. Then Rand-Mason complicated the affair. Kimball had a murder on his back and I scared him. He thought we had enough to convict him or that we'd get it. He said to himself, 'I'm for it, anyway. I'll have to die. Well, why shouldn't my death hang Sandford?' And he played that last card."

"I suppose so," Lomas agreed. "In a way it's all quite rational, isn't it?"

"I always said it would be. Grant that it was worth anything to ruin Sandford and Kimball's a most efficient fellow. But why was it worth anything to ruin Sandford?"

"Ah, God knows," said Lomas gravely.

"Yes. I wonder if Jane Brown does." He handed Lomas a letter.

"DEAR SIR,—your advertisement for information about Mrs. Ellen Edith Sandford. I have some which is at your service if you can satisfy me why you want it.—yours truly, JANE BROWN."

"I should say Jane is a character," said Lomas.

"Yes, she allured me. I told her who I was and she said she'd come to tea."

She kept her appointment. Reggie found himself facing a large young woman. In her construction nature had been very happy. She had decorated its work with admirable art. She was physically in the grand

145

style, but she had a merry eye, and her clothes were not only charming but of a sophisticated elegance.

Reggie, there is no doubt, stared at her for a moment and a half. "Miss — Jane — Brown," he said slowly.

"I haven't brought my godfathers and godmothers, Mr. Fortune," she smiled. "But I am Jane Brown really. I always felt I couldn't live up to it. I see you know me."

"If seeing were knowing, I should know Miss Joan Amber very well. It's delightful to be able to thank her for the real Rosalind — all the Rosalind there is."

She made him a curtsy. "I'm lucky. I didn't think you'd be like this. I expected an old man with glasses and — — "

"This," said Reggie maliciously — "this is the Chief of the Criminal Investigation Department — Mr. Lomas."

Lomas let his eyeglass fall. "I also am young enough to go to the theatre. I shall go on being young so long as Miss Amber is acting."

"May I sit down?" said she pathetically. "You're rather overwhelming. I thought it would be terrific and severe and suspicious. But you know you are bland — simply bland."

"This is your fault, Lomas," said Reggie severely. "I have often been called flippant and even futile, but never bland before — never bland."

"It is a tribute to your maturity, my dear Fortune."

Her golden eyes sent a glance at Reggie. "Mature!" she said. "I suppose you are real? Oh, let's be serious. I am Jane Brown, you know. Amber — of course I had to have another name for the stage — Amber because of my hair." She touched it.

"And your eyes," said Reggie.

"Never mind," said she, with another glance, but the gaiety had gone out of them. "My father was a doctor in Liverpool. He is worth twenty thousand of me, and he never made enough to live on. A poor middle-class practice, the work wore him out by the time he was fifty, and now he's an invalid in Devonshire. He can't walk upstairs even — heart, you know. And he simply pines to work. Oh, I know this doesn't matter to you, but I can't forget it. If only people were paid what they're worth! I beg your pardon. This isn't business-like. Well, he was the doctor the Kimball family went to. Old Mr. Kimball was a clerk, and the son, the man who was drowned the other day, began like that too. The old people died about the time young Mr. Kimball and his sister grew up. She kept house for her brother. He began as a broker and got on. In a way—my father always says that—in a way he was devoted to her. Nothing he could pay for was too good for her. He always wanted her with him. But he made awful demands on her. She mustn't have any interests of her own. She mustn't make any friends. Like some men are with their wives, you know. Horrible, isn't it?" She turned upon Reggie.

"Common form of selfishness. Passing into mania. Not only male, you know. Some mothers are like that."

"Yes, I know they are. But it's worst with men and their wives."

"The wife can't grow up. The children can," Reggie agreed.

"It is exactly that," said she eagerly. "You understand. Oh, well, this isn't business-like either. Ellen Kimball fell in love. He was just an ordinary sort of man, a clerk of some sort—Sandford was his name. Horace Kimball was furious. My father says Sandford was nothing in particular. There was no special reason why she should marry him or why she shouldn't. He was insignificant."

"Heredity." Reggie nodded to Lomas.

"I beg your pardon?"

"Your father understood men. Miss Amber."

"Indeed he does. Of course Horace Kimball did the absurd thing, said she mustn't marry, abused Sandford, and so on, and of course that made her marry. Unfortunately—this really seems to be the only thing against her—unfortunately she was married in a sly, secret sort of way. She didn't tell her brother she'd made up her mind, or when the marriage was to be or anything. She simply slunk out of his house and left him to find out. I suppose he had terrified her, poor thing, or his bullying made her sullen," said Miss Amber. "It was rather feeble of her. Only one hates to blame her. Her brother was furious. My father says that he never saw such a strange case of a man holding down a passionate rage. He thought at one time that Horace Kimball would have gone mad. The thing seemed like an obsession. Doesn't it seem paltry? A man wild with temper because he was jealous of his sister marrying!"

"Most jealousy is paltry." Lomas shrugged.

"Jealous of his sister marrying," Reggie repeated. "Yes, I dare say seven men in ten are. Common human emotion. Commonest in the form of mothers hating their sons' wives, Miss Amber. Still, men do their bit. Fathers proverbially object to daughters marrying. Brothers — well, there's quite a lot of folklore about brothers killing their sisters' lovers. Yes, common human emotion."

"I think jealousy is simply loathsome," said Miss Amber, with a quiver of her admirable nose. "Well, it's fair to say Horace Kimball seemed to get over the worst of his. He just lost himself in his business, my father says. He wouldn't see his sister again, not even when her child was born (it was a boy). He simply swept her out of his life. Even when Sandford got into trouble, he wouldn't hear of helping her. My father quarrelled with him over that. He said to my father, 'She's made her bed, and they can all die in it'. Oh, I know he's dead, and one oughtn't to say things. But I call that simply devilish."

"Yes, I believe in the devil too," said Reggie. "Devilish! You're exactly right, Miss Amber. Sandford got into trouble, did he? What was that?"

"It was some scandal about his business. A breach of trust in some way. His employers didn't prosecute, but they dismissed him in disgrace. My father doesn't remember the details. It was giving away some business secrets."

Reggie looked at Lomas. "That's very interesting," he said.

"Interesting! Poor people, it was misery for them. Sandford was ruined. My father says he never really tried to make a fresh start. He just died because he didn't want to go on living. And his wife broke her heart over it. She seemed like a woman frightened out of her senses, my father says. She got it into her head that it was all her brother's fault, that he had planned the whole thing. It was absurd, of course, but can you wonder?"

"I don't wonder," said Reggie.

"She was deadly afraid of her brother. She made up her mind that he would be the death of her baby too. So she ran away from Liverpool and hid in a little village in North Wales, Llanfairfechan, and nobody knew where she had gone. She had a little money of her own, and her husband had been well insured. She had just enough, and she lived quite alone in a cottage off the road to the mountains, and there she died. My father says her son did rather well. He got scholarships to Oxford, and my father

148

fancies he went into the Civil Service, but he lost sight of him after the mother died."

"I'm infinitely obliged to you. Miss Amber," said Reggie, and rang for tea.

"Oh, no, don't! I always thought that poor woman's story was too miserably sad. I don't know why you wanted it — no, no, I'm not asking — but if it could set anything right, or do anybody any good, it seems somehow to make it better. It wouldn't be so uselessly cruel."

"Over the past the gods themselves have no power," Reggie said. "We can't help her, poor soul. I dare say it's something to her to know that her son is safe and making good — in spite of all the devilry."

"Something to her — of course it is!" said Miss Amber, and looked divine.

"There's that," said Reggie, watching her.

"You won't mind my saying professionally that you have been very useful. Miss Amber," said Lomas. "You have cleared up what was a very tiresome mystery. I was being bothered. That's a serious disturbance of the machinery of Empire." He succeeded, as he desired, in setting the conversation to a lighter tune. He made Miss Amber's eyes again merry. He did not prevent Reggie from looking at her. "You must promise me another opportunity to thank you," he said, as she was going.

"Dear me, I thought you had been doing nothing else," said she demurely, and looked at the table and made a face. "Oh, Mr. Fortune, what, what a tea! I leave all my reputation behind me. Men hate to see women eat, don't they? But do men always make teas like this?"

"I've a simple mind. I live the simple life."

She looked at him fairly. "You said simple. Do you know how I feel? I feel as if I hadn't a secret left all my own," and she swept away. He was a long time gone letting her out.

"And that's that," Reggie said when he came back.

"Really?" Lomas was dim behind cigar smoke.

"All quite natural now, isn't it?"

"My dear fellow, you knew it all and you knew it right. You told me so. Kamerad, kamerad."

Reggie lit his pipe. "Jealously, hate, mania. He broke the man the girl married. Curious that affair, wasn't it? Even the great criminal, he runs in

149

a groove, he keeps to one kind of crime. The same dodge for the son that he used for the father. Then either he lost track of the mother or he preferred to hurt her through the son. He was an epicure in his little pleasures. The son came along. I dare say Kimball took that department because the son was in it. And then he was ready to smash everything for the sake of his hate—damage his own career, do a filthy murder, die himself, if he could torture his sister's child. Yes. The devil is with power, Lomas."

"I fancy you annoy him a little, my dear Fortune. But how can you believe in the devil? You have just seen—her."

Reggie smiled. "She is a woman, isn't she?"

"I think you might act on that theory. When is it to be?"

"Lomas, old thing, you're not only bland, you're obvious. Which is much worse."

THE END

Other Murder Mystery titles by Affordable Classics

The Daffodil Mystery by Edgar Wallace (ISBN 979-8736685820)

The Dead Letter by Metta Victoria Fuller Victor (ISBN 979-8730075870)

The Leavenworth Case by Anna Katherine Green (ISBN 979-8715577955)

The Circular Staircase by Mary Roberts Rinehart (ISBN 979-8705496570)

Mr Fortune's Practise by H.C. Bailey (ISBN 979-8707381232)

The Mystery of the Yellow Room by Gaston Leroux (ISBN 979-8598212530)

The Mystery of a Hansom Cab by Fergus Hume (ISBN 979-8574343302)

The Last Stroke by Lawrence L Lynch (ISBN 979-8564781343)

The Case of Jennie Brice by Mary Roberts Rinehart (ISBN 979-8569454693)

That Affair at Elizabeth by Burton E Stevenson (ISBN 979-8554774522)

The Brand of Silence by Johnston McCulley (ISBN 979-8698488620)

The Cask by Freeman Wills Crofts (ISBN 979-8695139884)

The Red House Mystery by A.A. Milne (ISBN 979-8680584439)

Made in United States
Troutdale, OR
08/17/2024

21933730R00094